WIFEY:
FROM MISTRESS TO WIFEY

WIFEY:
FROM MISTRESS TO WIFEY

ERICA HILTON

This is a work of fiction. All of the characters, organizations, and events portrayed in this novel are either products of the author's imagination or are used fictitiously.

www.melodramapublishing.com

Library of Congress Control Number: 2011927238
ISBN-13: 978-1934157466
ISBN-10: 1934157465
First Edition: November 2011
10 9 8 7 6 5 4 3 2 1

Interior Design: Candace K. Cottrell
Cover Design: Marion Designs

CHAPTER 1

Jasmine

I t was one in the morning on a Friday, and I had been sitting in Shabazz's condo since ten o'clock that night. I was bored and broke, a combination that always turned me into a brat and a bitch. What made matters worse was, Shabazz wasn't picking up his phone nor returning any of my text messages, so I didn't know what the fuck was going on.

I did know, though, that I was getting tired of his bullshit and his disrespect. I was tired of playing with my pussy and watching movies by myself and falling asleep while waiting on his ass to come home from running the streets. I knew Shabazz was going to come home wanting to fuck, and then after we fucked, he was going to have a new excuse about why his money wasn't right. And, more than anything, I was way past tired of hearing why his paper was fucked up.

When I heard the keys jangling in the lock, I put the remote control down, stood up from off the couch, and walked toward the front door, where I stood with my bare feet, wearing my pink wife-beater and my black leggings. I had my hands on my hips, in a defiant position. I was ready for war, ready to confront Shabazz and have him explain to me why he couldn't at least return a fucking text message.

I shouted at Shabazz as soon as he pushed open the door, "Can you tell me why the fuck"—I paused in the middle of my yelling, and my mouth fell open. I couldn't believe what I was seeing.

Shabazz hobbled into the living room, his hands, his shirt, his pants, and his sneakers all covered in blood.

"Oh my God! Baby, what happened? What happened to you?" I asked, panicking as my heart pounded through my chest.

"Them LeFrak niggas killed Skeen!" Shabazz was hyperventilating as he spoke. He stripped down to his underwear as quickly as he could.

"Are you serious? Did you get hurt? What happened? They shot you?" I tried my best to see if I could tell where the blood was coming from.

Shabazz dropped to one knee, wincing in pain.

"Nah, but I think I broke my muthafuckin' ankle!" he said and yelled out in pain. In frustration he punched his living room floor three times and left a bloodstain on the white oak hardwood floors in the process.

At that point Shabazz's phone started to vibrate, but he didn't pick it up.

"Baby, just chill and try to relax. I'll take care of you." I ran off to the bathroom and grabbed some towels and hydrogen peroxide. By the time I came back to the living room, Shabazz was on his feet and limping toward his bedroom.

"Baby, what are you doing? I told you to just chill! Look at your leg!"

"Jasmine, I gotta get dressed. We gotta get the fuck up out of here! I don't know what's up, but something ain't right. I can feel it.

It's like niggas set us up or something."

"Shabazz, calm down! Look at your leg. Just sit for a minute and let me clean that out first."

Shabazz turned his head and saw the gash in the back of his thigh. He shook his head, his lips curled in anger. "I got grazed and didn't even feel that shit!"

"This won't burn, but it'll help clean it out so that it won't get infected." I poured peroxide onto one of the towels and then applied it to the gash.

Although Shabazz was wincing in pain, I could tell that he was finally starting to calm down. But, at the same time, he was still very much on edge and kept saying that we had to hurry up and leave his condo.

"You wasn't answering your phone or your texts or nothing. I mean, I see why now, but oh my God! What the hell happened? Tell me everything. You scared the shit out of me, coming in here covered with blood like that!"

"My ankle is killing me."

At that moment his phone began vibrating, and it seemed like it wouldn't stop.

"You not gonna answer your phone?"

Shabazz looked at me, but he ignored me. I had him sit down on the couch, and then I went and got a bucket and filled it with water and ice so he could soak his foot and his ankle in it. After a few minutes of having his foot in the ice water, he finally began to tell me what had happened.

"We was out in Pomonock all day, and around nine o'clock, I hit up Skeen and told him to come through with the re-up. He was in Brownsville when I hit him up, so he didn't get to Queens until after eleven. So when he gets to the building, he called me, and I came down and met him outside in front of his truck, and we both walk back into the building together. But when we get into the lobby, I see this nigga name Brandon from LeFrak posted up on the wall near the elevators, and he's like, 'Yo, Skeen, you know what this is,' and he pulls out the ratchet and aimed that shit at us."

"What did Skeen do?"

"Skeen looked at me like, '*What the fuck!*' I knew by his look that he wasn't strapped, so I ain't even hesitate. I pulled out my burner and I go to let off, but my shit jammed."

"What?" I asked in disbelief.

"Exactly. So I'm like, '*Ahhh, fuck!*' and I start backing up to get the fuck out of Dodge. I was still tryin' to fire, but the shit just locked up on me. Then Money just starts letting off at me and Skeen—*Blaow blaow blaow blaow!*—and the gun blasts is echoing and ricocheting and shit, like crazy, in the lobby. So I dip around to the other side of the elevators, made it into the stairwell, and ran up like three flights. And the whole time, I'm trying to fire my shit to un-jam it, and it finally fires.

"As soon as I knew it was firing, I was straight. I ran back down the three flights and I tripped. That's when I fucked up my ankle. By the time I get back to the lobby, I see Skeen laid out in front of the elevators, bleeding crazy, and he was barely moving but his eyes was open. By that time Brandon and his punk ass was gone, and people started flooding into the lobby to see what happened.

"I picked Skeen up and he was spitting up blood, and he had that look like he knew he was about to die. I carried him to my truck and put him inside, and I fly to Jamaica Hospital. When I got there, I grabbed a wheelchair and I pulled him out of my truck and put him in the wheelchair. Then I wheeled him in, and I just left him in the lobby of the emergency room, and I bounced."

"You bounced?" I asked, not fully understanding why.

"Yeah, I had to. With my probation, my ass would be locked up. I couldn't take the chance."

"Y'all had beef with this dude or something?" I asked.

"Nah, I mean he's from LeFrak, and LeFrak niggas always bump heads with Pomonock niggas, so that's nothing. But he probably watched how we move and he caught us slippin.'" Shabazz shook his head.

"So it was just a stickup?"

"Yeah, whatever. I mean, I don't know. He got the re-up, so it seems like a stickup. But, at the same time, that shit seemed like a setup."

At that point his phone began vibrating again. And when it stopped, it started again. It seemed like it wasn't going to stop vibrating until he answered it.

"This muthafucka Nico! I don't wanna hear this nigga's bullshit." Shabazz reluctantly answered the phone. "Yo!" he shouted into the phone after putting it on speaker mode. His hands still had dried-up blood on them, and I figured he didn't want to get the blood on the phone.

I nursed his ankle while he spoke.

"Shabazz, you a'ight? Where's Skeen? Niggas been blowing up my phone telling me y'all got shot. What the fuck happened?"

"I don't wanna talk on the phone. Where you at? I'll come through."

"Don't worry about where I'm at! What the fuck happened to Skeen?" Nico barked through the phone.

"I dropped the nigga at Jamaica Hospital. He ain't make it, though. I could tell he was gone before we even made it there."

Nico was quiet, and I could just sense his anger through his silence.

Shabazz spoke up. "Skeen came through on a re-up, and Brandon caught us slippin'," he explained.

"Nah, the nigga caught YOU slippin', homie! All I know right now is Brandon is s till breathing, you still breathing, and Skeen ain't breathing and my product is missing. What the fuck is wrong with that equation?"

"I put it on everything, my gun jammed on me, and that's the only reason he let off on us like that."

"Shabazz, you fuckin' up, my nigga! Skeen's uncle is coming home in two days, and now how the fuck I'm gonna tell him some shit like his nephew just got murdered?"

Shabazz and Nico both were quiet.

"If your shit jammed and you a real G, then you take a fuckin' bullet! That's how you was supposed to get down. But, from what I hear, niggas is telling me that yo' ass ran like a bitch and left Skeen."

Shabazz took the phone off speaker and put it to his ear and began talking. "That's not how it went down," he replied.

I couldn't really hear what Nico was saying, but I definitely could tell that he was barking on Shabazz.

"A'ight, yeah. A'ight, I'll be there. No doubt," Shabazz said before ending the call with Nico.

Shabazz didn't immediately say anything to me, and I didn't say anything to him. The vibe in the room felt similar to the awkwardness of seeing your friend getting screamed on by one of their parents.

Shabazz tossed his phone across the room.

I watched it bounce off the floor. "Don't stress out, baby," I said as I continued to nurse his ankle.

I did my best to front and to be a voice of encouragement, but all I could think about was what a difference six months made. Six months ago when I had first met Shabazz, I was feeling him from the moment I saw him. He had a bald head, his goatee was perfectly trimmed, and he had the whitest teeth I had ever seen. And his white teeth complemented his smooth, dark skin perfectly. Shabazz was pushing an all-black Spyker SUV, his swagger was on a thousand, and from day one it seemed like we fucked each other twice a day every day like two rabbits in heat.

It was all good because it wasn't like I was letting him fuck for free. Shabazz would trick off on me, and he always made sure that I wanted for nothing. But recently that all started to change, and in the last month or so, it seemed like his money, his swagger, and his street cred were all starting to quickly dry up.

Shabazz ran both of his hands down his face. I could see that he was in physical pain and that he was also feeling punked, stressed, and anguished, all at the same time. There was no way at that moment that I could possibly bring up the fact that I was broke and needed some cash. I needed tuition money, car insurance money, clothes money, and spending money.

I knew I needed to rethink this situation. Perhaps it was time to start looking for a new sponsor.

CHAPTER 2

Nico

Two days after Skeen was killed, his uncle Bebo came home from prison after doing seven years in Club Fed on a conspiracy charge. But years before going to jail, Bebo had started a Brooklyn-based drug crew that he called "Ghetto Mafia."

Back when he'd first started Ghetto Mafia, I was a teenage low-level, hand-to-hand drug dealer in the organization, but I eventually worked my way up to a crew chief and then to a lieutenant. Ultimately, I became Bebo's right-hand man and the number-two person in the organization. And when Bebo got locked up seven years ago, I took over the head position and had been holding it down ever since.

If I'm being real, I can say that Bebo didn't know what the fuck he was doing before he went to prison and that's why he got locked up. I mean, he was street-smart, and he had more heart than anybody that I had ever met. The only problem was, Bebo never had the business smarts that he needed to mix with his street smarts. Me, on the other hand, I had the heart, the street smarts, and the business mind to match.

When Bebo got locked up, we was controlling most of Queens and half of Brooklyn, but now, seven years later, we ran the New

York City drug game, moving heroin, cocaine, and marijuana in ten different states on the East Coast and three states in the Midwest. When I took over the organization, we went from grossing 8 million a year to now grossing 1.5 million a month.

With the money we were making, it was nothing for me to make sure that Bebo came home to a brand-new Bentley coupe that was parked and waiting for him in front of Touch nightclub on 52nd Street in Manhattan, which was where I'd decided to throw his homecoming party.

It was around nine-thirty at night when I arrived at Touch with my fiancé Mia, and my swagger was heightened. My driver opened our door, and we stepped out of our Maybach Landaulet in style. I was wearing a $4,000 tailored suit that I had custom made specifically for this party. Mia was wearing a form-fitting black-and-silver Gucci cocktail dress that showed off her ass. And she wore it with high heels that showed off her toned caramel legs.

As we exited our car and made our way past the line that snaked down the block from the front door of the club, Mia and I looked like New York royalty and the ultimate power couple.

With my hand firmly on the small of Mia's back, I ushered her into the party, avoiding any pictures.

"Nico, what's good?" one of the bouncers said to me as he removed the velvet rope to let me and Mia go inside.

I gave the bouncer a pound, and I told him to make sure that he escorted Bebo, as soon as he arrived, directly to area we'd be lounging in.

"As soon as Bebo gets here, make sure you let him know we got them bottles on deck for him in the back."

"No doubt," he replied.

"Hey yo, make shit feel like the fucking President is walking up in this muthafucka when he arrives. You feel me, my nigga?"

"I gotchu," the bouncer reassured me.

I quickly looked around to see if I saw any dudes who looked like they were on some jealous-hating shit, but from what I could see, everybody looked like they were there to party in peace.

"This is a real sexy spot, baby," Mia said to me as she held on to my arm and we made our way fully into the spot.

DJ Pro Styles was doing the music, and although it was still early and the spot wasn't fully packed yet, I knew it was going to be a good night. Pro Styles had everybody that wasn't at the bar out on the dance floor enjoying the music, and the energy in the spot was perfect.

Before long, different members of Ghetto Mafia started arriving, and we all made our way over to a private area that I had reserved specifically for Bebo's arrival. When he arrived, I wanted him to feel the respect, and the unity and the love. Mia mingled with the wives and girlfriends of the other Bebo members, and I made sure that nobody popped any bottles until Bebo arrived.

We didn't have to wait too long because about a half an hour later Bebo arrived in the private lounge area that we had set up. He was with ten other dudes; two of them I had never seen before.

"My muthafuckin' nigga! Welcome home, my dude!" I said into Bebo's ear after giving him a pound and what seemed like a two-minute-long ghetto embrace.

Bebo grinned. "You did my shit up right!"

"We just getting started. You know how I do!" I replied. I then introduced Mia to Bebo, whom she had never met in person.

"I finally get to meet you. Nico talks about you like you his blood brother, so I feel like I already know you." Mia smiled her perfect smile, gently shaking Bebo's hand.

"This is my brother right here!" Bebo replied to Mia and gave me another pound. "I got so many wild stories I could tell you about this nigga right here!" He laughed.

Before I could blink, Bebo was surrounded by everybody coming up to him and showing him love.

"Nico, I wanna build witchu, give me a minute though," Bebo said to me.

I nodded my head in response.

Mia then commented to me how Bebo was much shorter than she had envisioned him being.

I didn't reply to Mia directly and told her, "Be right back." I had to go check on something with the promoter. Mia chilled and continued to mingle with everybody, and I walked off to try and find out what was up with the stripper chicks I had hired to be with Bebo for the night.

While I eased my way to the front of the club trying to find the promoter, I bumped into Shabazz. He had a bad-ass thick chick on his arm, and he was also with a drug dealer in our organization from Pomonock named Poota.

"Ohhh shit! What up! What's good! My nigga Nico in the muthafuckin' house!" Shabazz said to me. The music was loud, and he had to raise his voice over the music, but he was being extra loud and unusually animated as he held out his hand for a pound.

I gave Shabazz a pound and a quick embrace. He reeked of liquor and weed. Right at that moment my short fuse was blown, but I maintained and didn't check him immediately.

"Poota, what up, baby pa'?" I gave him a pound.

The sexy chick Shabazz was with extended her hand to me and introduced herself. "How you doing, Nico? I'm Jasmine," she said without a hint of a smile.

I shook her hand and said hello and I was trying to figure out what vibe she was on.

"Yo, Nico, let's get these bottles poppin'!" Shabazz shouted.

I looked at Shabazz and was a split second from snatching his ass up and pimp-slapping him. I thought his girl sensed what was up by the look on my face.

"Excuse him for being so rude," Jasmine said. "You see I had to introduce myself. Where are y'all at?" she asked me, vying for a distraction. "Upstairs or in the back?"

I replied and told her that we had the whole club but that we were about to do a toast for Bebo in a private lounge in the back.

"Poota, take Jasmine with you to the back. I wanna holla at Shabazz real quick." Poota gave a head nod and walked off with her.

"Yo, they got nothing but asses up in this muthafucka!" Shabazz said to me while looking at a girl in a tight dress walk by.

"Shabazz, I killed niggas for showing me less respect than what you showing me right now!" I barked.

Shabazz frowned and had a look of confusion. He held his hands up as if to ask what I was talking about.

"How the fuck you coming up in here fucked up? What the fuck is you thinking?"

"We partying!"

"Nigga, you supposed to come up in here on the humble. Skeen got murked on your watch, your numbers is down, and you coming up in here high like shit is all good? Word up you better drop all that

animated shit and sober up real quick and maintain, muthafucka!"
I barked. "The wolves could be up in here itchin' to put your fuckin'
lights out and you're ready to give them your head on a platinum
platter! You a hard-headed muthafucka."

Shabazz still had that confused look on his face, but I said what
I had to say. I walked off to find the promoter. I was done with
explaining and talking to that nigga. We were partying for Bebo's
homecoming, but that didn't mean we could afford to be reckless. A
party like that was intoxicating for all stickup kids from the Bronx
to Brooklyn, just waiting for a quick come-up. Our soldiers—such as
Shabazz—had to always be alert. But that dumb muthafucka comes
in the spot high as a kite and all off-point and then sits up next to the
nigga whose nephew he let get killed?

Everybody in Ghetto Mafia knew how I got down. I ruled with
an iron fist, but that didn't mean that niggas didn't try me. Goons
were always lurking just waiting to catch me slipping, but I rarely, if
ever, got caught without my burner.

I found the promoter, and he told me that the girls were coming
in from New Jersey, that he had just spoken to them and they were
about twenty minutes away.

"Don't bullshit me."

"Nico, I got it. I'm on it. I'm good money," the promoter replied.

"Twenty minutes?" I asked and I glanced at my Audemars Piguet.
"Get them bitches here in ten," I demanded.

"OK," the promoter said, and without hesitation he got on his cell
phone and started making phone calls.

After I had squared that away, I went back to the lounge we had.
Now it was twice as packed as it had been before I'd left. People were
snapping pictures, and cocktail waitresses were taking orders.

Bebo was sitting down on a couch, next to Shabazz. From a distance I could tell that Shabazz was back to his drunk, animated bullshit and was trying to be the center of attention.

I had already had the promoter set up a wireless mic for our area, and the mic was linked to the speakers in the lounge Once the wireless mic was turned on, it would override the music coming out of the speakers so that only what was coming out of the mic would be heard. I turned on the mic and got everybody's attention.

"Yo, Bebo, come to the mic, homie!" I shouted into the mic.

Bebo stood up from the couch and came over to me, and he gave me a pound.

"Everybody know why we here. We all in here celebrating this dude Bebo right here. Fuck all them fantasy stories and lies that these rappers be talkin' in their music about so-called gangstas and all that Hollywood shit. When you talkin' 'bout New York, there ain't no name that rings out more than Bebo. And that's because Bebo is the realest nigga in New York. He's the best whoever did it! This is a real G right here, and we celebrating his homecoming. And be clear, so everybody understands, he just did seven years and he did them numbers with honor! A lotta niggas nowadays be snitching, and copping pleas and all that bullshit, but that ain't even in Bebo's DNA! Believe that! So everybody get a glass, a bottle, a drink or something, so we can do a toast to my nigga."

I reached and a grabbed a bottle of Dom P champagne. I waited and watched as other champagne bottles were popped and liquor was poured into all the glasses in the room. After about two minutes I popped open the bottle of champagne I had in my hand, and Bebo popped open the bottle that he had, and we tapped bottles.

"Welcome home, fam!" I said into the mic.

Everybody started to tap their champagne glasses and bottles.

Some chick screamed out, "Welcome home, Bebo! I love you, baby!"

I then turned off the wireless mic, and the music came back blasting through the speakers.

"I got some shorties coming through for you real soon," I said directly in Bebo's ear and I handed him a brand new $800,000 watch that was worth more than the one that I was rocking.

Bebo hardly acknowledged the expensive gift. He nodded his head, and then he took me off to the side and we started to talk.

"You on that shit with my nephew, right?" he asked.

"Definitely."

"This party, the Bentley, the Audemars Piguet, the chicks, that's all good, but I wasn't supposed to come home to no news like that."

"I gotchu, man. I'ma handle it," I assured him. "I put that on my life."

Bebo nodded his head, and then he pointed out the two dudes who came to the club with him.

"What you think about eating off the same package with different crews?"

I hesitated for a second because that wasn't something that I expected Bebo to say.

"You talkin' 'bout them cats right there?"

Bebo nodded his head and placed a toothpick into the corner of his mouth, but he didn't say anything.

"I mean, I don't know. Why? What's up?"

"We'll talk. Just think on that," Bebo replied, the toothpick still resting in his mouth.

I turned and saw Shabazz with a bottle of champagne in his hand, two-stepping to the music.

"Yo, I gotta put this nigga the fuck out," I said to Bebo. "The muthafucka coming in your shit fucked up. I already told this nigga to sober up and maintain. The hit squad could be in this bitch! Everybody needs to be on point."

Bebo cut his eyes toward Shabazz. "I thought this was my muthafuckin' party?" he asked. "This dude actin' like he got something to celebrate."

I nodded.

"We might have to count down his days..." Bebo continued.

I was way ahead of him. "Let me go holla at Mia. Enjoy your party. I got this." I walked over to Mia. "You see that chick over there?" I pointed in Jasmine's direction.

Mia nodded yes.

"Her name is Jasmine. Go holla at her, introduce yourself to her and walk her out to the bar upstairs or to the bathroom or something."

Mia knew not to question me about any moves I was making. Flashing her supermodel smile, she walked over to Jasmine and held out her hand. Jasmine smiled. The two of them began talking after shaking hands. After about three minutes I saw Mia walking out of the lounge area with her.

I began pushing my way aggressively through the crowd until I found Shabazz.

"Yo, get your shit and get the fuck up outta here!"

"What?"

"Shabazz, you heard what the fuck I said! Bounce, muthafucka!"

"I been maintaining."

"Muthafucka, I already told you your numbers is down, Brandon is still breathing, so you don't need to be partying. You need to

21

bounce and go put some work in. Ya feel me?"

Shabazz looked at me. Then he started to look around as if he was looking for his chick, or for somebody to come to his aid.

"My girl will make sure Jasmine is a'ight."

Shabazz quickly nodded his head once, and then he slowly backed off and put the champagne bottle down on one of the tables before walking off.

Not much longer after that, the promoter arrived with the stripper chicks from Jersey.

"That's you right there," I said to Bebo, pointing in the direction of the scantily clad girls standing across the room.

Bebo gave me a pound. "That's what's up. You know I don't need no introduction," he said before grinning and walking over to the other side of the room.

I wasn't a big champagne drinker, so I got the attention of one of the cocktail waitresses and asked her to bring me a bottle of white Hennessy. After a few minutes the waitress came back with my bottle, at almost the same time that Mia and Jasmine returned. Jasmine wasn't immediately looking for Shabazz, so I played everything cool and didn't mention anything about me putting him out of the club.

I nodded my head to the music and thought about the moves I had recently made and all of the new moves I had to make to stay on top.

CHAPTER 3

Mia

I t had been a little over a week since Bebo's homecoming party, and during that week, nobody had heard from or seen Shabazz. We didn't know if he had been murdered or if he had gotten locked up or what. I had met and exchanged numbers with Jasmine at Bebo's party. Nico wanted me to reach out to her and try and feel her out to see what was going on with Shabazz, telling me not to make things seem obvious or make her suspicious, just in case her man was talking to the feds or something.

I dialed Jasmine's number, and she picked up after the fourth ring.

"Hi, Jasmine. This is Mia," I said, trying to sound as cheery as possible but still sound like my normal reserved self.

Jasmine paused for a second and didn't say anything at first. I could hear music in the background. She turned the music down and then started to talk.

"Oh, Mia, what's up? I'm sorry. I thought I had locked your number into my phone, but I must not have, 'cause I'm lookin' at the number like, 'Whose number is this?'" Jasmine said with a tone that sounded genuine.

"Mmm-hhhmm. Let me find out you screening calls," I joked and said softly.

Jasmine laughed.

"Listen, I was calling you because I wanted to find out about the nursing program that you in. You was saying it's only a fifteen-month program?" I asked.

"Yup, fifteen months, but it's full-time though. Why you ask?"

"'Cause I need to get off my butt during the day. I mean, after I leave the gym in the morning, I'm home all day, and it's not like I got kids or anything, so I was like, I should just look into it and start it and try to just knock it out."

Jasmine seemed distracted and was quiet for a second before responding. "Yeah, you should. 'Cause if my non-studying-always-partying ass can pass these classes, you'll be fine."

"OK, so listen, you said you in SUNY Downstate in Brooklyn, right?"

"Yup."

Jasmine put me on hold for about a minute because she had another call. And while I waited I started to fix myself something to eat.

"Mia, let me call you back in about an hour," Jasmine said to me when she came back to the phone.

"All right, but real quick, do you have class today? Because I wanted to drive down there and speak to somebody in admissions or something, but I won't have a clue where I'm going."

"Wow! You really ain't playing," Jasmine said to me. "Yeah, actually I have a class that starts at eleven, and I'll be out at twelve fifteen, so if you want us to link up, that would be the best time."

"That's perfect." I told Jasmine I would get dressed and head to

Brooklyn and hit her up when she got out of class.

After I hung up the phone, I ate and then got dressed. I chilled with Nico for about an hour before I hopped into my Range Rover and headed over to SUNY Downstate. I was coming from the North Shore of Long Island, so by the time I got to Brooklyn, it was just approaching twelve noon. When I got there, I sent Jasmine a text message, so she would know where I was at.

Jasmine sent me a text right back and told me to just chill in my car on Clarkson Avenue and that she would be there in ten minutes. So, to kill time, I went to Starbucks and got a caramel macchiato and some shortbread cookies, and then I headed back to Clarkson Avenue and waited for Jasmine.

After about five more minutes of waiting I saw Jasmine looking around, so I rolled down the passenger side window and tapped on my horn until I got her attention.

"Jasmine!" I shouted out the window.

Jasmine saw me and came over to my truck.

"Hey," I said.

"Hey," Jasmine said, mockingly. "Do you always speak like that?"

"Like what?"

"So softly…almost like a baby. I gotta strain to hear ya ass."

"Excuse me? Am I missing something?"

Jasmine gave me a half smile. I didn't know what it was, but it was like I could sense some kind of mood change or some kind of hate on her part. I wasn't sure what it was, but she definitely was coming across different than when we spoke on the phone earlier.

"Nah, you good. I'm just busy."

"I really appreciate this. I didn't mean to catch you off guard and just call you out the blue," I added.

"No, it's OK," Jasmine said to me, not looking me square in my face. She rolled down the passenger side window and stuck her head out of the window and she looked into the side view mirror and began examining her eyebrows.

I discretely sent Nico a text message and told him to call me in five minutes.

"This your truck?" Jasmine asked, a hint of stankness in her voice.

I looked at her and nodded my head yes. Jasmine didn't say anything else after that.

"So, you were saying it's a full-time program?" I asked.

"Yeah," Jasmine said, sounding totally uninterested, looking at her cell phone and chuckling before sending someone a text message.

"Listen, I got my next class in twenty minutes, but you don't really need me. All you have to do is go into this building right there. Find a legal place to park first, of course, and then go into this building and ask the security guard where the admissions office is at and then get a brochure of the program and an application," Jasmine stated.

"Oh, OK," I replied, trying my hardest to figure out why Jasmine's mood had changed.

Right then my cell phone rang and it was Nico and I picked up on the second ring.

"Hey, honey," I said into the phone.

"Everything good?" Nico asked.

"I'm good. I'm here at SUNY Downstate in Brooklyn with Jasmine."

"I'm not on speaker phone, am I?" Nico asked.

"No, but listen, let me run in here and get this stuff, and I'll call you back when I'm heading back out."

"You straight?"

"Yes, babe," I replied.

"You can't really talk right now?"

"No."

"A'ight, so hit me back."

"OK, I will," I said before hanging up.

"Nico told me to tell you what's up," I said to Jasmine as soon as I hung up the phone.

Jasmine quickly asked me, "So you good?" totally ignoring what I had just said, preoccupied with her cell phone.

"Jasmine, are you OK?" I asked.

Jasmine nodded her head and looked at me. She had her hand on the door handle as if she was ready to bounce.

"Hold on, Jas." I reached over and grabbed hold of her arm. "Everything good with you and Shabazz?"

Jasmine paused in her tracks. She looked at me as if she was now trying to figure me out. "It is what it is. Why you ask?"

"I asked because I haven't seen him around, Nico hasn't seen him or heard from him, and I'm just sensing that you and him might be going through something, that's all."

From the look of her body language, Jasmine seemed to relax somewhat. She took her hand off the door handle, which I used as my opening to keep talking and prying for information.

"So y'all are going through some shit, right?"

"I mean, we ain't really goin' through nothing major, but it's just that the nigga be on some bullshit sometimes, and I can't figure him out."

"On some shit like what? What do you mean?"

"Like the other day he was talkin' 'bout how the game ain't in him no more and how he wants to leave the streets alone. And I'm tryin'

27

to talk to him like, 'Nigga, what the fuck!' It ain't like he can just up and get a corporate job somewhere or something. He keeps saying he wants to leave the streets alone, but he don't have no plan B. I can't figure the nigga out, but it's like he ain't the same thorough-ass dude I met." Jasmine shook her head. "This is just between me and you, *right?*" she added.

"Jasmine, you don't even have to say that to me." I reached and grabbed hold of the Macchiato I had been drinking and drank some before continuing. "I'm so rude! Excuse me," I smiled and said. "Do you want something to eat? Something to drink? My treat. I'm in here just steady munching and drinking in your face."

"Nah, I'm straight," Jasmine quickly replied.

"See, me and you, we need to hang out, because I totally know what you're saying and where you're coming from because your man and my man are from the same world, so I get it," I added with a slight half of a smile.

Jasmine looked at me and nodded her head. I opened up the small pack of shortbread cookies that I had also gotten from Starbucks and started to eat one.

Although Jasmine's man and my man were from the same world, me and Jasmine were from two different worlds when it came to sophistication. Jasmine was more of a loud but pretty hood rat chick with a ghetto edge to her. And I was more of the quiet good girl, middle class model type of chick that understood the hood and how to maneuver in it. But one thing that I knew for certain was the universal language of money. Nonchalantly I went into my bag, took out three stacks of hundred dollar bills, and handed them to Jasmine.

"What's this?" Jasmine quickly asked me with a confused smile.

"It's for you."

"Yeah, but what it is for?"

I took another bite of my cookie and drank some more of the Macchiato. "When I told Nico I was meeting up with you, he told me to give that to you."

Jasmine started to count the money. Although she was quiet as she counted it, I could literally feel the energy inside the truck change from negative to positive.

"Take the money and use it to take Shabazz somewhere nice. Go to Atlantic City or Canada or somewhere. I don't know, but just do something one-on-one with him and help him get his head right."

After she was done counting, she said, "Mia, this is three grand."

"Jasmine, you're family. This is what we do. Shabazz got a lot on his head right now with Skeen's murder, and everything is getting to him. So you could talk to him now like you been doing, but he probably won't hear you. And all it'll do is keep you frustrated. But if the two of you get away for a few days where you and him are one-on-one with no distractions, that's how you'll be able to connect with him and help him get his mind right. Trust me. I've been there before."

Jasmine was quiet. I could tell her wheels were turning.

"I been there with Nico. Not with Shabazz," I laughed and said. "You know what I mean, right?"

Jasmine was still quiet and she didn't crack a smile or nothing.

"Jasmine, like you just said to me, I'll say it to you—All this is between me and you. Shabazz don't have to know nothing about this money or us talking or anything." Then I added, "That three grand is student loan money or Pell grant money. You understand?"

Jasmine kept looking straight ahead, sort of like she was day-dreaming, and then after about thirty seconds or so, she looked directly at me and told me that she understood. She looked at her phone and noted the time.

"You know what? Fuck that class. Fuck all these classes. Find a place to park, and I'll come with you to the admissions office," Jasmine said to me, a sinister look on her face while she stuffed the money into the front pocket of her tight jeans.

I smiled and soon ended up finding a place to park.

Jasmine and I did make it to the admissions office, but Jasmine had no idea that I could have cared less about a nursing curriculum or about the prerequisite classes a person needed before entering the program. The only thing I wanted was to fulfill the mission Nico had given me, which was to gain Jasmine's trust.

After we left the admissions office, I took Jasmine to downtown Brooklyn and I treated her to lunch and to multiple apple martinis. By the time I dropped her back off at her car near the school late that afternoon, I was more than confident that I had fulfilled my mission.

"See, this is some goddamn bullshit right here," Jasmine said, referring to her car. She was slightly slurring her words, due to all the liquor she had drunk. "You see this rental that nigga got me driving? I look too good to be pushing a fuckin' rental!" Jasmine screamed out at the top of her lungs, sounding like a brat. "And to make matters worse, the car has to go back any day!"

"Jasmine, you are so crazy. You had one too many of them martinis. You sure you can drive?"

With an intoxicated look, she leaned over and gave me a hug. "We family, right?" she asked, totally random and from left field.

I smiled. "Jasmine, let me drive you home, and you can take a cab back over this way tomorrow for your car."

"Nah, nah, nah, I'm good," she replied, and then she started to make her way out of my truck.

"You sure?"

"Yeah, I'm good."

"I'll call you later," I said. "And we have to *really* hang out next time."

Jasmine looked at me and nodded her head. She waited for me to pull off before walking to the driver's side door of her car.

When I reached the red light, I looked in my rearview mirror and saw Jasmine pulling off from her parking spot. I smiled and turned on the radio and then I called Nico and filled him in on how everything had gone with me and Jasmine.

My assignment had been completed.

CHAPTER 4

Jasmine

Three days after I had linked up with Mia and got the money from her, I decided to use some of it by surprising Shabazz with something he loved and was passionate about. Shabazz was the biggest boxing fan in the world. He was always talking about boxing and always watching it, so I decided to take him to MGM Grand at the Foxwoods Casino in Connecticut to watch the WBC welterweight championship fight between Ortiz and Berto.

"I knew I should've bet on this fight. Ortiz and his punk ass don't got no chin. Didn't I tell you it wasn't gonna go past six rounds?" Shabazz asked me as we sat in a restaurant waiting for our food to arrive after the fight had ended.

I smiled and said, "You really know boxing."

"I love it!" Shabazz replied. "I need to teach you how to throw your hands." He playfully reached across the table and touched my chin with his hand.

"Wait until we get back in the room so we can slap-box. I'm nice with mines. Don't sleep on me." I joked.

Shabazz drank some of the rum and Coke he had ordered.

"So did you expect this to be your surprise?" I asked.

"Front row seats to the fight? Nah, I ain't expect this. It was a good surprise, though."

As soon as Shabazz finished saying that, our waitress arrived with our food. I had ordered shrimp alfredo, and Shabazz had ordered two lobsters with wild rice.

"Can I get you anything else?" the waitress asked us.

I was fine, but Shabazz took the liberty of ordering me another Hpnotiq, and he ordered himself another rum and Coke.

"You trying to get me drunk or something?"

Shabazz nodded his head once, and then he put some of his rice in his mouth.

I reached for my fork and twirled some pasta on it. I placed the food in my mouth.

"I don't know how you eat that Alfredo sauce," Shabazz said to me. "That shit is like eating warm milk and mayonnaise."

I chuckled at his remark. Just then I heard my phone vibrating and reached into my bag and got it. I saw that it was a text from Mia.

Why does it seem like whenever I Really need some, my man ain't home? Is it just me or what??? Lol. What's up, Jasmine? Just hollering at you.

I couldn't help but laugh out loud a little bit when I read the text. I was also actually kind of surprised that Mia would send me a text like that. We didn't know each other all that intimately, and she seemed more like the prim and proper, conservative supermodel type.

I put some shrimp on my fork and I ate some and then I responded back to Mia's text.

Hey girl. Trust Me, it's not just you. Lmao. We in Foxwoods right now, can't really talk. I'll hit you up when I get back.

I put my phone away and refocused on my food. "So is your lobster good?"

"Who was that?" Shabazz asked.

"That was Mia. She's crazy, and I thought she was a goodie-goodie type chick."

"When the fuck y'all get close?" Shabazz asked, a frown on his face.

"We exchanged numbers at Bebo's party. Is that a problem?"

"Give me your phone."

"For what?"

"Give me your fuckin' phone!" Shabazz said, drawing the attention of the people sitting in close proximity.

"Shabazz, you causing a scene, and I'm tryin' to figure out what the fuck for."

"Jasmine, hand me your muthafuckin' phone right now!" Shabazz stood up.

I handed him the phone just to get him to sit down and calm down. He took hold of the phone and started to go through it. I had the iPhone, and Shabazz didn't, so I knew he didn't know what he was looking at.

"Show me the text she just sent you."

"Oh my fuckin' God!" I slid my chair away from the table and stood up and went around to the other side of the table and brought up the list of text messages so Shabazz could read them.

"I guess we back in high school again, with this childish shit." I sat back down. "You really gonna stand there and read my texts? This is some bullshit!" I was definitely starting to lose my temper.

Shabazz handed me my phone back, and he sat down. "Delete her number from your phone."

"No! Why should I?"

"Because I fuckin' said so!" Shabazz shot back, accidentally causing some of his spit to hit me in my face.

I had to consciously pause and count to ten because I knew I was a split second from throwing my plate of food in his face. "OK, can we just rewind back five or ten minutes and start over? We was having a good time, and I don't want no stupid shit messing everything up."

At that point people around us still had their eyes on us because it was obvious that me and Shabazz weren't in lovey-dovey mode.

"Is everything OK?" our waitress asked as she approached our table.

Shabazz remained quiet, and I spoke up and told her that we were fine and didn't need anything.

"Now I see where all that talk you was doing earlier was coming from," Shabazz stated.

"All what talk?"

"About Skeen's murder, and if my money was straight, and all that shit!"

"Baby, that was just regular conversation I was making because you ain't been yourself, that's all."

Shabazz didn't say anything. Our little getaway was now fucked up, and we probably weren't even going to end up spending the night. I also remained quiet and tried to eat some more of my food, but at that point, my appetite was shot.

"OK, look, if you want me to keep it real with you, Mia reached out to me, and it was just about school. She was asking me about the nursing program I'm in. Did your name come up? Yes, but it's normal for her to ask me how you were doing."

"Hey, yo, do me a fuckin' favor," Shabazz said, pointing his two fingers at me. "Don't let my name come out your mouth. I don't give a fuck who you talking to! You feel me?"

I closed my eyes and I paused in frustration. I picked up my drink and drank some of it, and then I told Shabazz that I understood where he was coming from.

"My business and what I do ain't got shit to do with you. You don't know shit, and you don't say shit."

My vex meter was now off the charts. I was never one to hold my tongue, and I wasn't going to start now. I definitely wasn't going to just sit there and let Shabazz talk to me like I was his daughter or some shit.

"Your business don't have anything to do with me. You right about that. But at the same time, you gotta also understand that when you just up and get out of reach with your people, then niggas get nervous. You know that's how shit goes."

"See, this is what I'm talkin' 'bout. How the fuck you know I been out of reach? A minute ago you said Mia called you about school, and now you giving me the remix!"

"And I also said that your name came up! That wasn't no remix! You know what? I can't do this with you." I stood up and reached in my bag, placed two hundred dollars on the table, and started to walk away.

"Jasmine! Jasmine!" Shabazz called out to me.

I turned around and stood in my tracks with my arms folded and just looked at him. There was no way I was going to go back to the table and sit down, tired of Shabazz and his bullshit.

Shabazz realized I wasn't coming back to the table, and he got up and came over to me, and we walked out of the restaurant, headed toward the casino area.

"There's a lot of shit going on right now that you don't know about, and you don't need to know about."

"You wanna know what I need to know about?" I asked.

Shabazz looked at me but didn't respond.

"I need to know that regardless of what's going on, that you'll take care of home." I began shaking my head and rolling my eyes. "Yeah, I don't live with you and all that, but you know what I mean, because the principle is the same! It's called security. And, honestly, Shabazz, you wanting to grab my phone, and barking on me about little trivial shit—you coming across real insecure. So when you're insecure and all private about shit, then you tell me what the fuck am I supposed to feel and think?"

Shabazz was quiet because he knew I was right and he had no comeback.

"I'm going up to the room. You coming?" I asked.

"Nah, I'm going to the craps tables. I'm gonna chill down here."

It was only Friday night, and we weren't scheduled to check out until Sunday morning. But I knew right then and there that I was checking out of the hotel Saturday morning and bringing my black ass back to New York.

Kim Kardashian was having a birthday party in New York on Saturday that I had been planning on going to. My good friend Carlos was one of the promoters of the party, so that meant VIP treatment all around. And with Shabazz acting like a straight bitch-ass, there was no sense in me missing it just to chill with him in misery.

CHAPTER 5

Nico

"What you thinkin' Fam'?" BJ asked me right after we left a meeting with Bebo and headed out to Manhattan. BJ was my underboss and the person I most trusted with my life.

"What I think?" I paused and said, being very deliberate with my words. "I think the nigga on some bullshit. We don't need no product, and we don't need no shooters. So what the fuck we need to partner with anybody for?" I replied as BJ chauffeured me toward the midtown tunnel.

"Exactly, my nigga! What's wild is, Bebo just came home, and he's like, 'Fuck it,' and just right back in the mix with shit," BJ said.

"That's that ego shit," I replied. "And that ego shit is bad for everybody. It'll fuck up everybody's paper. What do I always tell you this game is about?"

"It's about buying shit for one dollar and selling it for two," BJ quickly replied.

"That's it. It's simple. Fuck the street rep 'cause when everybody knows your name, it means the feds know your name too. Bebo still on that late nineties shit, and that era is gone. But the muthafucka trapped in that shit. His frame of mind is fucked up."

"So how you gonna play it?" BJ asked.

I sat back in the passenger seat and I turned up the volume on the Jadakiss freestyle that was playing in the CD player. I slowly shook my head but I didn't reply to BJ's question simply because I wasn't sure how I was going to deal with Bebo's plan to partner with other drug crews.

Twenty minutes later, BJ and I found ourselves inside Club Amnesia, which was on 29th Street in Manhattan. We were both real cool with DJ Clue, who had told us to pass through the club, since he was doing the music for Kim Kardashian's birthday party. By the time we made it in the club, it was close to two in the morning, and the spot was rammed. The block was looking like a scene straight from a movie or some shit.

Clue had his man meet us at the front entrance, and he got us inside. Then we snaked our way through the club until we made it to a packed VIP area.

"Yo, I ain't with this Hollywood shit," I said to BJ.

"We'll chill for about an hour and then bounce," BJ replied into my ear over the music.

The VIP area was too packed for me, so I headed over to the bar area, while BJ posted up and chilled where he was at. BJ had a tool on him, but I wasn't strapped ,so I wasn't feeling all that comfortable.

I had been near the bar for no more than five minutes when some chick came up next to me.

"I know you're gonna buy me a drink, right?" she said, a smile on her face.

It was dark in the club, so I couldn't really see her face that well. At the same time, she did look familiar.

"Nico, it's Jasmine," she said.

"Oh shit! What's good, ma'ma'?" I replied, finally realizing who she was.

"Nothing. I'm just up in here with my girls." Jasmine replied. "These are my friends, Simone and Jada."

At that moment DJ Clue threw on Lil Wayne's hit song, "If I Die Today."

"Ahh yeah, this my shit right here!" Jasmine yelled out. She put one of her hands in the air and started dancing in front of me to the music.

"I didn't recognize you. But, yeah, I gotchu. Whatchu want? Tell your friends I got them too," I said while pulling out a large wad of cash, all hundred dollar bills.

"We been drinking Nuvo the whole night, so just get us that," Jasmine shouted into my ear.

I got the bartender's attention, and I ordered a bottle of Nuvo, a bottle of coconut Ciroc, and a bottle of Hennessy Paradis.

A young lady who had been sitting down at the bar got up, and Simone sat in her seat.

The bottles arrived, and Simone poured the drinks for everybody. I drank the Hennessy, and they drank the Ciroc and the Nuvo.

"Who you in here with?" Jasmine asked me.

"BJ," I replied.

Jasmine gave a look of contemplation.

"You know BJ, right? That's my man."

"I don't know him like that, but I know who he is."

I drank some of my drink, and then I sat my glass down on the bar. "What's up with your boy?"

"Shabazz?" Jasmine rolled her eyes and shook her head.

"What's up with that look?"

Jasmine shook her head again but didn't immediately reply.

"I don't really know. I can't figure him out." Jasmine then took some of the Nuvo and mixed it with the Hennessy and drank some. "We was up in Foxwoods last night, and we was gonna stay there for the weekend, but I had to bounce today. I couldn't deal with his shit for the weekend. I just couldn't take it."

I nodded my head and didn't say anything in response to what she was saying about Shabazz.

"I see you trying to get fucked up tonight," I said directly into Jasmine's ear. "You ain't playing fair with that dress you got on either. You might catch a murder charge 'cause you killing 'em in here."

Jasmine blushed. She started to bounce her body to the music, staring at me with a flirtatious look as she danced. Her two girlfriends told her that they would be back in a few minutes and that they were going to check on some dude named Carlos.

"So where you from, Jasmine?"

"Southside, near a hundred and ninth and Guy R. Brewer." She kept dancing with her drink in her hand, only now she was slightly backing her ass into me.

"Oh, so you a Queens girl." I drank some more liquor while Jasmine continued to dance.

As she kept dancing, she turned and faced me. "I'm originally from Prospect Heights in Brooklyn, but we moved to Queens when I was around twelve."

I nodded my head to acknowledge what Jasmine was saying while I looked at my phone and saw a text from Mia, asking what time was I coming home. I hit her right back and told her that I wasn't sure, and then I put my phone away.

"What you doing when you leave here?" I asked Jasmine.

Jasmine appeared surprised by my question and looked at me. "I really didn't think that far ahead. I guess I'm going home, right?"

I said into her ear, "Why don't you come to my spot near the FDR Drive and chill with me?"

"Come chill with you?" Jasmine turned around. "What, at your crib?" She stopped dancing.

I nodded my head yes.

"So Mia can stab my ass?" She then drank some more of her Nuvo.

I didn't respond to Jasmine's comment. I just looked at her and waited for her to tell me what she was going to do.

At that point Rick Ross's hit song came on, and everyone in the club started to get amped. And so did Jasmine.

"They playing all my shit tonight!" Jasmine then turned her ass back into me, and she grabbed my right hand and made me hold on to her stomach and waist while she danced.

"We good," I whispered into Jasmine's ear, and then I kissed her on her neck as she kept grinding on me. The liquor had my head feeling nice, and all I was thinking about was taking her back to my spot and smashing that ass.

Jasmine tilted her head back. "We good?"

"We grown, right?"

Jasmine nodded her head up and down, and then she turned and looked at me.

I wasn't playing games, and the straight look on my face said so.

"I drove here, and if I leave, my girls ain't gonna have a way to get back," she explained to me.

I nodded my head and then thought for a moment. Then I spoke into Jasmine's ear because the music seemed like it had gotten louder.

"It's all good. I gotta drop BJ back in East New York. So after you drop your girls off, we can link up."

She nodded her head. "OK, take my number."

I put her number into my phone, and after we finished our drinks, we parted ways. I went to look for BJ, and Jasmine went to look for her home girls.

It was a little past two thirty in the morning. In about two hours I was more than likely going to be fucking the shit out of Shabazz's girl.

CHAPTER 6

Mia

It was four in the morning. I was still up because I had gone to the John Legend concert with one of my girlfriends, and after dropping her off in the Bronx, I didn't get back to my house in Long Island until two in the morning and I wasn't that tired. I was lying in my bed and I had just turned off the TV when I heard my doorbell ringing, and I also heard knocking coming from the front door.

The first thing I thought was, Nico had lost his key or something. I dismissed that because I knew he would have called me if that was the case, and I hadn't heard from him since I'd sent him a text a few hours earlier.

"Who is this at this time of night?" I said out loud to myself as I got out of the bed and threw on my short black silk robe.

The banging got louder as I approached the door, making me a little bit nervous. I paused in my tracks, turned and ran back to my bedroom. I quickly switched on the closed-circuit television monitor, so I could see who was at the door. The motion light in front of my house had come on, but it was still too dark for me to clearly see who it was at the door. But I could definitely tell it was two guys.

I grabbed my phone and immediately called Nico. I called him two times in a row, and it rang out to voice mail each time.

"Answer your fucking phone!" I said in frustration as the knocks at the door got louder and louder.

I called Nico back, and again his phone rang out to voice mail.

Whoever it was at the front door, they were being very persistent, like they weren't going to go away. I looked at the television screen again, and this time I was able to tell that the two guys were definitely Spanish guys.

I tried calling Nico again, but I got no answer.

At that point I was beyond nervous. I ran to the closet to look for the small .22 handgun Nico had bought for me. I was frantically rummaging through the closet because I forgot exactly where I'd stashed it. And while I was looking I heard a loud bang coming from downstairs, and then I heard talking and feet moving. My front door had just been kicked in. My heart was in my feet.

I finally felt the steel from the gun. It wasn't the .22 I was looking for—it was Nico's chrome .45. With each heartbeat my heart felt like it was leaping out of my chest.

"That muthafucka ain't in here," I heard one of the Spanish dudes say from downstairs. After he said that, it was like everything went silent for a moment, and the only thing that could be heard was the pounding of my pulse as I stood stiff, my body frozen against my bedroom closet door.

I heard some movement on the first floor of the house and then I heard what sounded like feet coming up the stairs. The whole house was dark, except for the light coming from my bedroom. I wanted to turn it off, but I couldn't take the chance because I didn't know where the two intruders were.

About a minute later, with my heart still pounding and my palms sweaty, I heard the floor squeak. Someone was near my bathroom, because the hardwood floors always squeaked when someone walked nearby. And right after I heard the floor squeak, my cell phone, which I had accidentally left on the shelf of my closet when I was looking for the gun, started to vibrate, scaring the shit out of me and causing me to fire the gun into the ceiling.

My own gun blast startled me. And right after my gun went off, I heard two loud gunshots coming from the hallway. Instinctively, I ducked down and stayed crouched down and started to fire my gun in the direction of my hallway. I fired three shots. I was ready to piss on myself from fear. The next thing I know, water started coming from the sprinkler system and the burglar alarm started to sound nonstop.

I didn't know what was going, but I thanked God because the sound of the alarm spooked whoever it was in the house. I could hear them running down the steps as if they were making their way out.

By this time the water from the sprinklers had stopped, but the alarm was still sounding. I grabbed my cell phone and realized I had missed a call from Nico and immediately called him right back.

"Pick up the phone! Pick up the phone!" I said, but it rang out to voice mail.

At that point I didn't know what to do. My first instinct was to call the police, but at the same time I didn't want them searching the house unless I had first checked with Nico.

I looked at the closed-circuit monitor in the room and saw the two dudes exiting the house. I wanted to inspect my property, but I was too scared that someone was still in the house, or that the two dudes who had left would turn right around and come back inside.

I decided to try Nico's cell phone again, and finally he picked up on the fourth ring.

"Oh my God, baby! Oh my God! Somebody just broke into the house! I was calling you!" I screamed hysterically into the phone, tears streaming down my face.

"What? Did they touch you?"

"No, I grabbed the gun and started shooting, and the alarm started ringing, and they ran off. Oh my God! Baby, just come home. I'm so scared. I wanna call the cops. I can't take this."

"You still got the gun?"

"Yes," I replied, my body still trembling.

"OK, lock yourself in the room. Don't call the cops. I'm calling my peoples right now and have them come to the house. They'll be there in ten minutes. I'm on my way to the crib too. I'm gonna hang up, but I'm gonna call you right back and I'll stay on the phone with you until I get there."

"OK, hurry up, baby. I'm so scared right now." I did as Nico had instructed me. I barricaded myself inside our bedroom.

I turned off the lights and held on to the gun with both hands. And just as I turned off the lights, the alarm stopped ringing, and there was this deathly silence that filled our 6000-square foot home. I paced back and forth for a moment before tiptoeing to the window and looking out, hoping to see something, but all I saw was the pitch blackness of the night.

As sad as the thought was, I knew Nico was probably with one of his side chicks at that very moment. I just prayed that, wherever he was and whoever he was with, he would leave and hurry up and get to me, so I could breathe again and feel safe.

CHAPTER 7

Jasmine

After I left Nico, I went to the bathroom. All of that liquor I had been drinking was more than ready to come out. There was a small line to get into the bathroom, so while I waited, I sent Simone and Jada a text asking them where they were at because I was ready to bounce. I made sure not to tell them why I was ready to leave, because it was none of their business, and with them and their dysfunctional asses, they would have just been on some cock-blocking, hating shit anyway.

Simone didn't text me back, but Jada did, and she told me where they were at. Carlos reserved a table and some bottles for us not too far from the bar where we had bumped into Nico at. So I made my way over to Simone and Jada, and as soon as I arrived I knew Simone wasn't going to be ready to leave.

"Oh my fuckin' God! Jada, please tell me she knows this dude from somewhere, or that's her secret boo or something," I said, referring to some dude that Simone was deep tongue-kissing on the dance floor.

"I have no idea! You know your girl," Jada replied.

I shook my head in disgust and disbelief. "Go get her because we leaving right now. I can't wait on her, fucking with these broke-ass niggas."

Jada walked over to Simone, but Simone was paying her no mind. After she stopped kissing the guy, she turned around and was backing her ass up into the dude. And while she was grinding on him, he hoisted a bottle of champagne into the air with his left hand. Although it was dark in the club, it looked to me like he had his right hand in Simone's pants.

"You believe this shit?" I said to myself. I looked at my phone to see what time it was.

When I looked up, I saw Carlos approaching Simone. I couldn't hear what he was saying, but it looked like he was barking on her. I figured she had probably been trying to make Carlos jealous. I walked closer to try and defuse any tension and to make sure that I personally told Simone that we had to leave.

The guy that Simone was dancing with asked her, "You know this dude?"

Before Simone could say anything, Carlos responded, "Money, niggas get murked for that shit!" Carlos took both of his hands and pushed the dude in the chest, sending him backward.

"Oh my God!" Simone screamed. "Carlos, it's not even that serious. We was just dancing!"

After the dude got pushed, people knew that some drama was about to unfold. Two bouncers approached the scene and tried to see what was going on.

I grabbed Simone and asked, "What the fuck are you thinking?"

"Jasmine, not now! All right?"

I didn't even have a chance to respond because all I heard was screaming. I saw Carlos crashing to the floor. The dude Simone had been dancing with had cracked him over the head with a champagne bottle.

At that point all hell broke loose. The bouncers knocked the dude to the ground and started stomping him out. Tables were getting turned over. People were running and screaming, and the bouncers were trying to get control. But they were actually making things worse because they took the melee as an excuse to just randomly knock dudes out.

Jada grabbed me and Simone by the arm. "Come on! Let's get the fuck outta here before they start shooting," Jada screamed.

"Nah, get the fuck off me! I can't just leave Carlos like that!" Simone tried to fight her way back to where Carlos was, so she could help him.

Jada wasn't trying to hear that. "Simone, come on! We gonna get trampled up in here. Let's go! Now!"

Jada was strong as shit. She continued to pull on me and Simone, until finally Simone relented and decided to head for the exits. By that point it seemed as if the entire club had realized that a fight had broken out, and everything became an absolute zoo.

Finally, me, Jada, and Simone found an emergency exit, and we made our way out of the club and to the parking lot. Though it was a little after three in the morning, all of 29th Street was swamped with people and swarming with police.

"You know that was some real whorish, ghetto-ass project shit you just pulled up in there and almost got us killed, right?" I screamed at Simone.

"Jasmine, just take me home. I don't wanna hear your shit right now."

51

"Well, you gonna hear my shit. You up in the club kissing some nigga in the mouth that you just met? And had the nigga all up in your pussy on the dance floor! Why didn't you just pull your pants down and let him fuck you right there?"

"Jasmine, I said I don't wanna hear your shit right now! Just take me the fuck home."

The parking attendant pulled the car to where we were standing, I paid him, and the three of us got in and pulled off, headed back toward Queens.

I'll be in Queens real soon. Give me like 45 minutes to drop them off and shoot back.

That was a text I sent to Nico just to make sure he knew I wasn't fronting. I didn't want to tell him I had just left the club because I didn't want to give him any reason whatsoever to change his mind about us linking up.

"Simone. Really?" Jada asked as she turned around in the front passenger seat and looked at Simone as we drove.

"Jada, I'm telling you just like I told Jasmine. I don't wanna hear this shit right now. Turn the fuck around, turn the volume up on the music, and leave me the fuck alone!"

Jada shook her head and turned and faced forward. But she threw another dart at Simone. Under her breath, she said, "Probably don't even know the nigga's last name."

"Fuck you, Jada!" Simone yelled from the back seat and then lay down and stretched out across the entire backseat of my father's Lexus, her eyes closed. She mumbled something else under her breath about a credit card, but she wasn't making no sense, and I was paying her no mind. I just wanted to get both of them home and out of my car, so I could handle my business.

Ten minutes later, Simone suddenly sat up and started talking about how she didn't feel well and felt like shit.

"Jasmine, pull over. I gotta throw up," Simone shouted over the music.

"Ahh shit! Hold it until we cross into Queens," I said. We were crossing the 59th Street Bridge, and the car was moving at a good rate of speed, so there was no way for me to just pull over.

"I can't hold it. Just pull over and stop the car!"

"Simone, where the fuck you want me to pull over to? Roll down the window and hang your head out and throw the fuck up!"

"Just stop the car!"

"Bitch, I can't! But, I swear to God, if you throw up in my father's car, I will whip your muthafuckin' ass!"

Two minutes later we were just about to cross into Queens and Simone started banging on the back of my chair and tapping on her window.

"Roll the window down, Jasmine. I can't wait no longer. I gotta throw up now, and this window won't go down. Hurry up!"

"Ahh shit! I don't know these buttons like that. Try it now!" I yelled.

The window still wouldn't go down due to the child safety feature that was unknowingly on.

"It's not working," Simone screamed.

"OK, OK. Two seconds and I'll be able to pull over," I yelled.

The next thing I knew, all kind of shit that looked like baked ziti that had passed through a blender was coming out of Simone's mouth and landing all over the backseat of my dad's Lexus.

"Aggghhhhhh! I'm gonna kill you!" I screamed as I turned around and watched Simone continue to puke in the car.

A long glob of spit was hanging from her mouth, and her eyes were teary. She looked like she was done bringing everything up.

The next thing I heard was the sound of screeching brakes, followed by the loudest crash and bang, and our car spun around two times before coming to a stop. The crash had tossed me and Jada around and caused us to bang heads with each other. Simone had also been tossed around. She slipped off the seat and landed shoulder first into her own smelly vomit.

"This is not happening! This did not just happen! Oh my God! I can't believe this! My father is gonna kill me."

"Jasmine, they blew the stop sign though," Jada said. "It wasn't your fault."

I just sat frozen behind the wheel and didn't say anything, both of my hands gripping the steering wheel.

"There is vomit in my backseat, and I just had an accident. And I got somewhere to go tonight! I don't believe this shit," I shouted.

The driver from the other car came over to my car and tapped on the window, asking if we were all right.

"What the fuck was you thinking?" I barked on the other driver after I opened my door. I got out and walked around to the other side of the car and surveyed the damage. "Urrggghhh!" I said, looking at the damage.

The driver was saying something, but I was paying him no mind as I walked away from the car and tried to figure out what I was going to do. I walked a few feet away from the car and called Nico.

"You need the address, right?" Nico asked me as soon as he answered my call.

I sucked my teeth. "Do you believe that some clown just ran a stop sign and wrecked the whole side of the car?"

"Miss, I didn't run the stop sign," the other driver said.

"Yes, you fuckin' did!" I shouted.

"You a'ight? You didn't get hurt, did you?" Nico asked.

"I'm fine, but my car ain't."

"You need anything? I can call my man and have him tow you to his body shop in Valley Stream if you need me to."

"No, I'll be OK. I think I can drive it. I'm just gonna call the cops and report it. If I can't drive it, I'll call you back," I said to Nico.

"A'ight, you sure you all right, though?"

I sighed once again in frustration, and then I lowered my voice so that Jada wouldn't be able to hear everything I was saying.

"Yeah, I'm sure. But I am disappointed though. This is definitely not how I wanted to end my night. I wanted to chill with you," I explained to Nico.

"We'll make it happen," Nico replied. "Yo, my phone is blowing up. I gotta bounce, but call me if you need me."

"OK," I said and ended the call. I couldn't help but feel frustrated.

As I prepared to deal with my car accident, I was definitely hoping that I would get another opportunity to link up one-on-one with Nico.

CHAPTER 8

Nico

When I reached my crib I ran inside and I found my four goons who I had sent to my house to make sure Mia was safe. Mia immediately ran and hugged me.

"You OK?"

Mia nodded her head rapidly. I could tell she was still shaken up.

"The crib is good. We checked it top to bottom," Earl said to me.

"They take anything? Mia, did you see what they looked like at all?" I asked.

Mia was so nervous, her body was literally trembling as I held on to her. She explained that she only could see the intruders on the surveillance camera and that they looked Spanish, but she couldn't really tell for sure.

"I don't think they took anything," Mia added. "But I don't know for sure because everything just happened so fast."

I went upstairs and looked around. Other than the bullet holes in the walls and ceiling, everything looked in order. I went into my closet and saw that my safe hadn't been touched. Then I went back downstairs to the main floor and looked around, and things looked cool. Some pictures and a lamp had been knocked over, and the front door was broken, but other than that, everything was good.

I checked the basement and could tell that nobody had been there, so I quickly made my way back to the main floor.

"Muthafuckas ran up in my crib with my girl up in here. Somebody is dying behind this shit!" I said, emphatically.

By this time it was five in the morning, and my right hand, BJ, showed up at my crib with his cousin Lorenzo, who we all called Lo. Lo was from Harlem, but he ran with us and never really fucked with Harlem cats. About fifteen minutes later Bebo showed up, Corey, and one of my best soldiers.

Everybody who I wanted to be there was there, so I sent Mia upstairs so we could talk without her being around and hearing more than she needed to hear.

"Nico, just give me the word on who you want me to hit and it's done," Corey said.

"I got a hundred thousand on the heads of the cats that ran up in my crib tonight. A hundred thousand for each body," I confirmed. "Put the word on the street."

At that point BJ signaled for me to walk with him, so we could talk in private. We left the crew sitting in my dining room, and me and BJ walked outside to the front of the house out of the earshot of everyone.

"The Colombians ain't fuckin' with us," BJ said to me, referring to our connect.

"What the fuck you talkin' 'bout?"

"On the way over here to your crib, Lo just told me that the Colombians think Bebo is a snitch and they ain't fuckin' with us," BJ explained.

"You just fuckin' with me, right?" I said with a smirk on my face. I tapped BJ on his bodybuilder chest with my fist.

"The word is, the feds just got Ren, and with Bebo just coming home, they putting two and two together and saying shit ain't a coincidence and wondering why he only did seven years and not more," BJ continued to explain. "That money we sent with Lo, the shit came back to us."

"The money for the last go-'round?" I asked.

BJ nodded his head.

"So we got no product, and our connect ain't fuckin' with us," I said.

"Exactly."

I kept quiet and thought to myself for a minute, and it was like BJ could read my mind.

"You thinkin' Bebo got his hand in this shit, right?" BJ asked me.

"Bebo could be snitching, and that's why he's been talkin' 'bout us eatin' off the same package with different crews. But he ain't been to my crib since he came home. Only a few niggas even know that I rest way out here." I paused in contemplation. "Shabazz sent them muthafuckas to my crib tonight. Put a bounty on his head. One hundred grand for the muthafucka that bodies him. Two hundred if he's brought to me alive."

BJ kept quiet, but Lo spoke. "You wanna put in your own work on that dude, right?"

"You already know how I get down." And so did Shabazz. I knew he was ghost and wouldn't resurface on my territory until he sang me a lullaby. I don't know what gave me away; maybe I was a little too aggressive at Bebo's party. See, I was the one who had orchestrated the hit on Skeen, and that was because from behind bars, Bebo was planning the ultimate takeover. He felt that he'd started Ghetto Mafia from the ground floor and when he got jammed up the streets forgot about him and the name Bebo was now replaced with Nico. Someone as egotistical as Bebo couldn't let that shit ride. He couldn't appreciate where I was taking our organization. Him and Skeen had been playing checkers and making moves that they thought I didn't know about. But the whole time that they were playing checkers, I was playing chess.

Shabazz, on the other hand, was too much of a wild card, and I had a strong feeling that once Bebo came home, him and Skeen would use Shabazz as the trigger man to take me out and take over the empire that I'd helped build.

Yeah, I was hoping that Shabazz would have gotten murked when Skeen got murdered. That was the plan, but it turned out not to be reality.

It was all good, though, because if the streets couldn't locate Shabazz, I knew I had a new sexy pawn in this chess game that I could use to get at him.

"So what about product?" BJ looked at me to see what I wanted to do.

"Give me a day, and I'll get you the name of these Haitian dudes out of Miami. I want you and Lo to go down there and chop it up with them, and that can be our new connect for right now until I sort out what the fuck is going on."

BJ looked at me and nodded his head. He gave me a pound before we went back inside my house, and I addressed everybody.

"Yo, something is definitely up. I need all y'all speaking to your people to see what they know or what they hearing and let's see what comes back about this shit. And let everybody know the hundred thousand is good money."

Everybody was clear on exactly where I was coming from, and nobody had any questions.

"And if y'all see Shabazz, tell that nigga to holla at me," I said, giving everybody a pound before they left my crib.

CHAPTER 9

Mia

A few days had passed since our house had been broken into. In the days that immediately followed the break-in, Nico had hired a private security firm to station an armed guard in front of our home on a twenty-four-hour basis. So I felt pretty secure whenever I was home or whenever I left to go out. But emotionally I didn't feel secure at all. In spite of everything that had happened with the break-in, Nico still wasn't immediately answering my calls or returning my calls right away. And whenever we were together, he rarely answered his phone or talked freely in front of me.

For the most part I had grown used to Nico's ways, and I knew he was really no different than a professional athlete or a celebrity—being a target of gold-digging women. Although I grew used to Nico's philandering ways, it was never something that made me feel good on any level. One way that I reasoned his infidelity was, I had always told myself, as long as I didn't see anything or as long as he didn't fuck with anyone I knew personally, then I could pretty much act like I didn't care, even though in reality I did care.

But that Wednesday following the break-in, there was something I couldn't just ignore, and that was a text message that Jasmine had sent to my phone. The text said:

Sorry again about Saturday night. Call me when you can. Stop hiding. LOL. Maybe we can link up today. And can you give me the number to your man's body shop?

I replied right back to the message and told her that she had sent the text to me by mistake. And it took her about fifteen minutes before she replied back to me.

LOL. I'm sorry Mia. You can delete that. That text was for someone else. So how you been?

I didn't respond back right away to Jasmine, but something in my gut told me that she meant to send that text to Nico and ended up sending it to me by accident. I knew Nico wouldn't let me look at his phone, so what I did was, I found a copy of an old Sprint bill and went online and logged into Nico's Sprint account. I'd secretly gotten his username and password a few months back when he'd inadvertently scribbled it on our light bill. I looked at the numbers he had called, and I looked at the numbers that had called him during the past couple of days.

As I scanned the phone numbers my heart was beating fast from anxiety. I was hoping I didn't see Jasmine's number. But, sure enough, I saw an incoming call from Jasmine to Nico right around the time my house had gotten broken into. And I also knew Nico was real cool with this white boy who owned a body shop, so it wasn't hard for me to connect the dots and know that Jasmine meant to send that text to Nico.

Immediately I just felt sick to my stomach, like I wanted to throw up. My mind was racing with all kinds of thoughts. I was wondering how long Nico had been talking to Jasmine. Was he fucking her? Had he played me by using me to deliver money to her? Was the money really for her personal pockets and not for extracting viable information about Shabazz? What did he see in her that he didn't see in me? Was it because she was in school and I wasn't? Was she the reason he hadn't taken me on any vacations recently?

I didn't know exactly what to say or what to do. And although I was a quiet person by nature, I was never a person to hold my tongue, and I wasn't going to start now. I didn't hesitate any longer and I called Jasmine to confront her.

Jasmine picked up on the second ring.

"Mia, I'm sorry about that text," she said, sounding like she was snickering or laughing as if things were funny.

"Jasmine, I'm not a dummy!" I shot back into the phone. I knew I caught her off guard.

"What are you talking about?"

"Don't play stupid. Are. You. Fuck-ing. My. Man?" I asked her in a cadence that stressed each syllable.

Jasmine was silent. I kept quiet too, waiting for her to blink first.

"You just joking with me, right?" she asked with a fake chuckle.

"Do I sound like I'm joking?" I asked and mocked her with a fake chuckle of my own.

"Mia, really? You're that insecure? I send you a text message by accident and you come at me like this?"

"Answer my question! Are you fucking Nico?"

"No, I'm not fucking Nico," Jasmine replied short and blunt.

"So why are you calling him at all times of the night?"

"Seriously, Mia? Like, are you really serious right now? OK, first of all, don't call my number with no bullshit like this. I don't care who you are or who your man is, you can't disrespect me!"

I could feel my ghetto side starting to rise up to the surface. "Ain't nobody disrespecting you!" I yelled into the phone.

"You calling my phone all outta pocket and cursing and shit. That is disrespect! And if you wanna know who your man is fucking, then you should ask your man. And don't call me no more with this bullshit, or we gonna have a problem!" Jasmine hung up the phone.

I was beyond heated and ready for war, so I called her right back. "Mia, stop calling my phone!"

"You broke-ass ghetto bitch! Let me tell you something—If I find out you called my man one more time, I'm whipping your little project ass!"

Jasmine started to laugh into the phone. "Whateva, Mia. I ain't hardly from the projects and I ain't hard to find. If I ain't at school, then I'm on a hundred and ninth avenue and Guy R. Brewer Boulevard, so whateva you wanna do, bring it. But you better come correct! And if I wanted your man, believe me, I could have him."

"Oh, now you talking real reckless I see?"

"Why are you still talking to me?" Jasmine screamed.

"You right. I'm done talking. But test me if you want to, bitch!" I hung up, abruptly ending the call.

I wanted to call Nico, but I didn't. I figured, if he was talking to Jasmine, she was going to let him know what happened, and if he said something to me, then that would be the confirmation I needed to know that he was actually fucking her.

I sat down on my bed, feeling like someone had just gutted me. But there was no way I was going to let that bitch take my man. She had no idea who she was fucking with.

CHAPTER 10

Jasmine

When the call ended with Mia, I was so vexed. I was definitely in fight mode and ready for war. At the same time, I realized I had fucked up by accidentally sending her that text message and I wanted to make sure that I hadn't put Nico in a bad spot. I had sent the text to Nico like I had initially intended to do but he didn't respond so I didn't know what to think.

I paced around in my motel room wondering what Mia was really going do. She seemed far from the rah-rah type, but at the same time I knew that it was always the quiet ones that you had to watch out for because they were the ones that would strike like a snake and catch you off guard. I called Simone just to let her know what was up.

"Get your sneakers and Vaseline ready," I said to Simone. This was the first time I had spoken to her since she threw up in my father's car that night. And I was still upset with her.

"You got beef?" Simone said without hesitation. Simone was all over the place at times and she pissed me off a lot, but she was my home girl for real and always had my back, no matter what.

"Yeah, this bitch named Mia, she just called my phone flipping the fuck out, talking about why I was calling her man and all that bullshit. She's like if I call her man again there's going to be a problem. So I was like, 'Bitch, you know where to find me. I'm right in the hood—a Hundred and Ninth and Guy R. Brewer Boulevard—and if I wanted your man, believe me I would have him.'"

"You ain't gotta say nothing else," Simone said. "I'm getting dressed right now."

"Nah, I'm not even home. Fuck her ass. I'm just saying be ready because if this bitch show up at my crib later on tonight or whenever on some bullshit I'm calling you."

"Oh, no doubt, I'm there. You know I got your back. But who is Mia? And who is her man?"

"Her man is Nico. You was probably too drunk to remember he was the one who bought us the bottle of Nuvo at the club the other night. He gave me his number, and I called him. These chicks kill me, always ready to step to the next chick, but it's their man that they need to be checking."

Just then I heard a knock at the door of my motel room. "Simone, I gotta go, but keep your phone on in case I need you," I said.

"Definitely."

I turned my phone off and put it away. There was another knock at my door. I paused to gather myself, blowing out some air from my lungs in an attempt to decompress. Mia had really worked my nerves, and I had a job to do, so the last thing I wanted was for my mind to be on drama.

After I was done gathering myself, I made it to the door and opened it after looking through the peephole.

"Hey, Chyna?"

"Yes. Hi." I tried to make my smile as natural as possible. Chyna was my escort name. "Mike, right?"

"Yes."

I could tell Mike was nervous, which always made me feel a bit more comfortable. That way it would help me feel a bit more assured that I wasn't dealing with a cop.

"So is this your first time?" I asked Mike as I closed the door behind him. I was wearing a nice form-fitted top, tight jeans, and black high heels.

"Yes, and no. Yes, it's my first time with a black girl, but no, it's not my first time."

I smiled then double-checked the door to make sure that it had definitely slam-locked.

"Oh, well, I feel special then. You know what they say. Once you go black, you'll never go back."

Mike laughed. I could tell he was starting to feel a bit more relaxed.

"Well, Mike, you can have a seat on the bed. You can get comfortable, and what I'll do is, I'll go into the bathroom and freshen up, and in the meantime you can put any gifts that you have for me right there on the table or next to the TV.

Mike nodded, indicating that he understood where I was coming from.

I made my way into the bathroom of the motel room I had booked for the day. It wasn't the nicest of motels, but it was located not too far from Kennedy Airport, which meant that I would profit more from the money I earned turning tricks and at the same time I didn't have to travel too far to get my money.

Nobody knew about my secret hustle, and there wasn't any way in hell that I would've ever told anybody how I got down. I rolled totally independent, so there was no one pimping me or none of that, and I planned to keep things that way. But, on the real, I hated each and every trick I turned and couldn't wait until I could find another way to maintain my lifestyle without working and going to school. As far as I was concerned, fucking for money wasn't the best option for me, but it wasn't exactly the worst either. And with Shabazz's unpredictable ass, it wasn't like I could definitely depend on him for cash, so I had to do what I had to do.

In the bathroom I quickly changed into my white stilettos, a white see-through thong, and a white see-through bra. I had already taken a shower, but as part of my routine with each john, I took a warm washcloth and slid it across my shaved pussy, and then I took some perfume and sprayed some on my chest, neck, wrists, and on my panties. I took some Scope mouthwash and swooshed it around in my mouth and then spat it out before exiting the bathroom.

"Wow! That's a transformation," Mike said.

I gave him a fake smile, but at this point I was strictly concerned with my money. I headed straight to the table, located on the opposite end of the room. The nine crisp twenty-dollar bills brought a real genuine smile to my face. Mike had paid for one hour's worth of pussy. I gathered the money and told him that he could get undressed. Then I walked back to the bathroom and placed the money in my bag. Afterwards I retrieved a condom, which I held in my left hand, and I also retrieved my cell phone, which I held in my right. I made a fake call to my voice mail and returned to the room, where Mike could see me on the phone, and asked him to give me one minute.

"Yeah. Yes, I'm OK," I said into the phone, acting like I was talking to someone. Just in case Mike was some psycho-ass serial killer, it would make him think twice. "One hour. OK cool," I added before hanging up the phone.

By this time Mike was undressed, and I walked over to him and told him to lay back and relax. Mike followed my instructions and laid on his back. I took the bottle of baby oil from on the nightstand next to the bed and poured some into my hands and rubbed them together before massaging Mike's chest.

"You are so beautiful," Mike said. "What nationality are you?"

"Oh, thank you. I'm all black. Parents are from the South."

I hated all this small talk shit, but I had to do it because that was how I built repeat clientele.

After massaging Mike's chest, I reached my hands behind me and took hold of his dick and began to stroke it.

"How old are you?"

"Nineteen, just like my Craigslist ad said I was. My birthday is next month. I'll be twenty on the fifteenth."

By this time Mike had closed his eyes and had stopped with all the damn questions. His dick was hard, and I was hoping that he hadn't been drinking, or that he wasn't one of those dudes who took forever to come.

"Can I kiss you?" Mike asked me.

I smiled and shook my head no. For the life of me, I couldn't understand why in the hell all of these dirty-ass dudes would want to kiss me. Kissing is part of lovemaking. We're fucking. Big difference.

"You can touch me, though." I took Mike's hand and guided it to my pussy.

He started to rub on my clit, but I wasn't the slightest bit turned on. I was just thankful that Mike was somewhat handsome, and he

71

smelled good, so those two factors helped me make like I was into it. At the same time I wanted to hurry up and get this shit over with.

I took the condom out of the wrapper, placed it in my mouth, and then I went down on Mike and placed the condom on his dick, using only my mouth.

"I never seen anyone do that in my life!" Mike said as I started sucking his dick.

"I bet I can show you another trick. How do you want it? Me on top? From the back?"

Mike told me he wanted me on top, so I quickly mounted his dick and slid it into my pussy and started riding him. As I rode him, I twisted my hips into him like I was dancing to reggae music, at the same time doing pussy-tightening techniques.

"You feel that?" I asked him.

Mike smiled a big Kool-Aid smile and nodded his head yes.

"You like my pussy, daddy?" I said directly into Mike's ear.

I leaned toward him and ran my tongue back and forth on his earlobe, while continuing to work my pussy. I could tell Mike was into it and loving my pussy because of the way he grabbed my ass and how hard he started pumping his dick in and out of me.

"Yes, daddy!" I screamed. I still wasn't into the sex like that, but dudes loved it when I made them feel like they were killing my shit. I had no problem being an actress.

As I continued contracting my pussy on his dick, I could feel he was about to come. I had to encourage him so that we could get this over with.

"You gonna come for me, daddy?"

"Oh yeah!"

"You gonna come in my black pussy? I wanna feel you come, baby."

I knew *black pussy* was all I needed to say for Mike to pop his cork.

"Uggggh! I'm coming! I'm coming in your fuckin' black pussy!"

I quickly got up because I never played that shit and let a dude come and then have him all up in my pussy. Anything could happen—a condom could break, come could leak out, anything. I got up and stroked his dick with my hand, so he could get the final effects of any tingling sensations running through his body.

"That was one of the best orgasms I ever had," Mike said to me as he lay on the bed breathing hard.

I got up from the bed and kissed him on the cheek and smiled. I didn't want to totally be rude, since I still was working on any tip that he might have wanted to throw my way.

"I hope that means I'll see you again?" I asked, hoping Mike would take the cue and leave.

Thankfully Mike was in a hurry and didn't want to come a second time. He tipped me twenty dollars, and we had about five minutes of small talk before he left to go home to his wife and kids. The twenty-dollar tip was OK, about ten percent. But nowadays even waitresses are tipped twenty-five percent or better.

Although it was early, I wasn't in the mood for no more clients, so I didn't bother to take out my laptop and run any more online ads. Instead I took a shower, got dressed, and called a cab to take me back home. On my ride home, I called Nico. I was going to call him from my regular phone, but instead I decided to call him from the prepaid phone I used for my escorting.

Nico's phone rang out to voice mail, but I didn't leave a message. I figured he probably didn't answer numbers he didn't recognize. I decided to just take my chances and shoot him a text message. I knew exactly how to test the waters.

Hey, Nico, this is Jasmine. When you can, give me a call I just wanted to tell you something about my man.

Five minutes after I sent that text, the cab was pulling up to my house, and my cell phone rang. It was Nico.

"Hello," I said, answering the phone.

"Jasmine, what's good?"

"Yeah, I just wanted to tell you that I don't really know what's going on, but just between me and you, the other night Shabazz came by my house for a quick minute and he was saying how you got him out here still on salary and starving while less loyal niggas is working on a percentage."

"He was telling you that? Where the fuck that nigga been at?"

"I don't know, but he was crazy, saying shit like, 'Hungry dogs ain't loyal because they'll eat you alive,' and it was just weird, like I never seen him like that before, I don't really know for sure, but you know how you get the feeling that somebody is scheming or something? Well, he ain't say no names, but I just get the feeling that somebody is plotting on you. I ain't saying it's him, but I'm just saying."

"Yeah, yeah, I feel you. I mean, I been trying to holla at the nigga, but he been ghost, you know what I mean? Shit is real fucked up out on these streets right now, and these cats that you thought was down with you, they be switching up sides," Nico replied.

"I been tryin' to tell him that he shouldn't just be outta reach the way he is, but just like I was tellin' Mia, I can't get through to him," I exaggerated and said.

Nico was quiet for a moment, and so was I.

Nico asked, "You know where he at right now?"

"Nope," I replied nonchalantly but truthfully. "He been in and outta town, but I don't really know where to."

"Yeah, a'ight, but if you see him, hit me up, a'ight?"

"OK, I will, and sorry if I caused you any drama from earlier with my text."

"What are you talking about?"

"I had accidentally sent Mia the exact same text I had sent you earlier about Shabazz," I lied. "And when I realized it was her phone, I told her to disregard, but she flipped the fuck out."

"And she called you?" he asked with a bit of an attitude.

"Yeah, she was buggin' out, cursing and threatening to come to my crib and all that. I was like, 'Waaow! Are you serious?'" I chuckled slightly, trying to make Mia seem like she had wilded out in an uncalled for way.

"When the fuck was this?"

"Today, not too long ago."

"If she went through my phone, I'll fuck her ass up for that ignorant shit!"

"No, it's OK. It's fine. I know you probably already got enough on your mind, so don't even bring it up. Mia probably just don't understand, unless she's a nag like that all the time," I said, trying my best to sound compassionate and still take a shot at her.

Nico didn't respond to me, so I continued talking, to keep the conversation flowing.

"I never did get up with you that night," I reminded him.

"That was on you."

"That was then, though. What's up with now?"

Nico explained that he had to shoot to Miami in the morning for Mia's photo shoot for J. Lo and that he would get up with me as soon as he got back.

"Oh, so she models? I did a couple of music videos, and I'm trying to get heavier into modeling," I told him.

"Yeah, that's what's up. Yo, I gotta bounce. I'll get with you, though."

"Oh, OK."

Nico randomly asked, "You still grown, right?"

"What did you say?" I could tell my smile was detectable through the phone.

"You know what I'm asking you."

I paused before replying. "I gotchu," I said with a slight chuckle.

Nico added, "That's all I needed to know," before we ended the call.

I was feeling flattered because I knew Nico wanted to sex me, and I couldn't wait to put it on his sexy ass. Plus, with Mia talking shit, it just gave me more incentive to fuck her man and prove I could have him if I wanted him.

CHAPTER 11

Nico

Although I was now living really comfortable on the North Shore of Long Island, I was originally from the streets of Bed-Stuy, Brooklyn. Since I was from the streets, I was familiar with South Jamaica, Queens, where I was headed to meet Jasmine so that I could bring her to my man's auto body shop to take care of the damage to her father's car. Jasmine had sent me a text message with her address, and I gave the address to my driver and reclined in the backseat of my all-black Maybach Landaulet until we reached 109th Avenue, right off Guy R. Brewer Boulevard.

"Jasmine, you live in a white house?" I asked just to confirm I was in the right spot. I had already circled the block to make sure Shabazz wasn't laying in the cut somewhere waiting to set my ass up.

"Yeah, on One Hundred and Ninth Avenue. One block from Forty projects."

"No doubt. So, yo, I'm outside your crib. You ready?"

"Give me ten minutes and I'll be right out."

From behind the curtain of my rear window, I was able to see when Jasmine finally came out of her house. She looked around to see where I was parked, but she had no idea which car I was in. I pulled back the curtain that hid my face from the public, rolled down the window, and called her name. I got her attention.

Jasmine quickly walked across the street. She was wearing a nice short black leather coat, jeans, and construction Timberland boots.

"Wow! Look at you, looking all presidential and e'rythang." Jasmine chuckled. "I love this car! Let me find out you a quarterback for the New York Jets or something." Jasmine knew I was getting money. "And I can't believe you got a driver!"

Ignoring her last comment, I asked, "So you got the car? I don't see it," I said through the window, not making a move to get out of my vehicle.

"Yeah, yeah, it's in the garage."

"OK, so pull out and follow my car. The spot ain't too far. It's on Merrick in Valley Stream, right near Rosedale." I turned my attention toward my driver. "Henry we're going to City Autobody. Also the Lexus with the pretty young lady will be following us, so be mindful."

"Yes sir."

It took us all of ten minutes to arrive at the body shop. When we arrived, Henry parked, got out and made his way to my door, and opened it for me. I walked up to Jasmine, who was in the driver's seat, parked behind my car, and told her to pull up to the bay off to the far right. After she did that, I signaled for her to turn off the engine and to come to me.

As Jasmine walked toward me, I couldn't help but notice and reconfirm just how sexy she was. The last time I had seen her, it was in a dark nightclub. She had looked good that night, but that night she was dressed sexier. I always liked when a chick could rock sweat pants and socks or any other regular-looking outfit like Jasmine was presently wearing and still look good. It was about one in the afternoon, and the sun was shining brightly, so I was able to get a really good look at what she was working with. I could tell that she had some hoodrat tendencies, but that didn't detract from the fact that she was just naturally beautiful and had a body that wouldn't quit. And she also had a sexy walk.

"You rocking Timbs just because I'm rocking 'em," I teasingly said to Jasmine. I had on a brand new pair of True Religion jeans, a brand-new long-sleeve button-up Burberry polo shirt, and a leather coat.

Jasmine smiled but didn't say anything.

As we made our way into the shop, I informed Jasmine, "My man Tony owns this spot. He's an Italian dude from Howard Beach. He's cool as hell. I already told him I was coming through with you."

Tony was sitting behind the counter along with one of the girls who worked the front counter. He was leaning backwards in a desk chair with wheels.

I said to Tony, "You keep leaning back like that, and you gonna buss your muthafuckin' ass."

Tony turned and saw that it was me. "Ohhh, Nicoooo! My man." He stood up and came from around the counter and gave me a pound and a quick embrace.

"What's the deal with you?" Tony said with his Italian accent. "You tell me two other times you were coming then I don't see you. I thought you took the car to somebody else."

"Nah, we just had conflicts trying to link up. Then I was outta town in South Beach for a minute, so you know how it goes."

"Tell me about it. I'm so friggin' busy in here, I don't even have time to count all the money I'm making," Tony joked. "Then I got the old lady always on my ass, nagging about something. It's crazy."

"Mo' money, mo' problems," I told him.

Tony nodded his head toward Jasmine, and when he got her attention, he said to her, "You see this guy right here? He's a good fuckin' dude. He's the best. I knew him since we were ten years old. We played basketball together."

"Oh, OK. That's cool. And y'all stayed in touch all these years?"

"You friggin' kiddin' me? This is like my brother. I'd trust this guy with my life."

Jasmine smiled.

"So, Tony, somebody fucked up, blew a stop sign, and hit her Lexus. I figured I would have her come check you and let you knock it out for her, since she was telling me that she had a two-thousand-dollar deductible with her insurance."

"Yeah, I got you. Let me see the damage. Is the car outside?"

The three of us walked out of the reception area and made our way outside to the car.

"How's the Maybach treating you?" Tony asked.

"Fuck what you heard. On the real, that's the best car on the planet. I love it. Much better than them small-ass Bugatti's niggas be pushing."

"You hear this guy? He's got more money than God!" Tony laughed. "OK. So this is the car? Wow! This can't be more than six months old," Tony stated, referring to the Lexus.

"It's not," Jasmine replied.

"Well, I can fix it, no problem. It looks like it's just the front quarter panel, but if you see right here where the passenger door got pushed in a little, it doesn't look like much. But if I redo the front quarter panel and leave the door like that, it'll look crazy. So, to do it right, I'll have to replace the front passenger door and the front quarter panel."

"OK, so what am I looking at?" I asked.

"For this, I'll bang the insurance company for eleven grand, and when they cut me the check, since you my nigga, I'll give you back the two grand she paid for the deductible." Tony laughed and told Jasmine not to take offense because I had given him permission to use the N-word.

Jasmine smiled at Tony's comment and nodded her head to let him know she was cool with everything he had said.

"I'm sorry, miss. Nico, this rude schmuck, didn't even introduce us. I didn't get your name." Tony extended his hand to Jasmine.

"I'm Jasmine," she smiled and replied.

"You have any questions for me?"

"No. Nico told me he would take care of the deductible for me, so I guess I only wanna know when it will be ready."

Tony stared at her for a moment before continuing to speak. "Did anybody ever tell you that you look—"

Jasmine cut Tony off and finished his sentence. "Like Jada Pinkett Smith, right?"

"No. I was actually going say the singer Mya."

"Yup, I get that too sometimes."

Tony said, "Jada Pinkett, she's skinny and got an ass like a white girl."

"Oh my God." Jasmine laughed at Tony and covered her mouth.

"Definitely you look more like Mya than Jada Pinkett," Tony said, chuckling. "But, to answer your question, today is Tuesday. I can have the car completed and ready for you by Saturday afternoon. Would that work?"

"OK. Yeah, that's not bad."

Tony paused and kept quiet and waited to see if anyone had any more questions, and since we didn't, he led us back inside and filled out paperwork that he had Jasmine sign.

When they were done with the paperwork, I reached into my pants pocket and pulled out a huge wad of cash. I always walked with fifteen to twenty grand in my pocket. I counted out twenty hundred-dollar bills and laid them out on the table. I hadn't even fucked Jasmine yet and I was personally giving her money, but it didn't matter though because, at the end of the day, it was just money. It was more where that came from so I wasn't stressing it like that.

"This guy couldn't wear those tight skinny jeans if he wanted to. All his cash wouldn't fit." Tony laughed as he scooped up the money off his desk and recounted it.

"Baggy jeans all day every day for me. I won't ever be on that skinny jeans gay shit."

I gave Tony a pound and thanked him for looking out for me and told him I would hit him up later, and then me and Jasmine left and headed toward my car.

"So whatchu doing for the rest of the day?" I asked as Henry held open the rear driver's side door for me. I instructed Jasmine to get in, which she did. Henry closed the door behind her, and then he walked around and opened the rear passenger door, and I got in and sat down.

"I'm just gonna chill. I don't have nothing specific to do. I already decided to skip my classes," Jasmine responded as the driver closed my door and made his way to the driver's seat.

I got my driver's attention and instructed him to take us to Benihana's on Northern Boulevard. He nodded his head, and we pulled off.

It was December, so it was way too cold for convertible drop-top flossing, but if the weather was warm, I would have really blown

Jasmine's mind by removing only the rear top and leaving in place the top for the front half where the driver was.

"My bad," I said. "I didn't even ask you if you wanted to go get something to eat."

"Yeah, definitely, and thank you," Jasmine immediately and eagerly responded.

"So how old are you?"

"I'm nineteen, and my birthday is next Saturday."

"So you'll be twenty?"

Jasmine nodded her head yes, and then it was like she wanted to purposely change the subject to anything but her age.

"This car is so comfortable, I could live back here, it's so roomy. I love it."

We continued to have more small talk until we reached the restaurant, which was a twenty-minute ride from the body shop.

"Chill," I said to Jasmine as I touched her leg. "The driver will come open the door for you then you can get out."

Jasmine followed my directions and didn't make a move to step out of the car until her door was opened for her. The same was done for me, and then we made our way inside the restaurant and were seated by the hostess.

We both took off our coats, so we could make ourselves more comfortable. The way the restaurant was set up, it was sort of like a large square table with a grill in the middle where a Japanese chef would cook and prepare the meal right in front of the diners.

So that I wouldn't be sitting too far away from Jasmine, I decided to sit right next to her instead of across from her. "You ever been here before?" I asked.

Jasmine shook her head no.

"Do you trust me to order for you?"

"OK," Jasmine said with a smile.

I ordered filet mignon and hibachi chicken for me, and hibachi steak and hibachi shrimp for Jasmine, and I ordered spicy tuna rolls. For drinks, I ordered sake for both of us.

The drinks were the first thing to arrive. Jasmine had never drank sake, and I was surprised that she liked it.

"You passed your first exam," I said.

"Oh really? And what exam would that be?"

"You're open to new things. I like that."

"That's what keeps life interesting." Jasmine then added, "You taught me something today."

"What's that?"

"That I shouldn't settle and I should set my standards real high for myself. I mean, to me it's hot that you got a driver opening doors for you and chauffeuring you around and drinking hard-to-pronounce drinks and all of that."

I laughed.

"No, I mean, really. I see shit like that on TV and it's always like, 'Oh, that's for the Donald Trump's and people like that,' but it can be for people who look just like me. It's just that I never see it, so I assume that it's not possible."

"I feel you. Life is all about what you expose yourself to. But you gotta have vision to see what other people can't see and then be relentless in pursuing it."

"I like that," Jasmine replied. "You sounding all educated and stuff. Let me find out you smart."

"I just got you by ten years, so it's more life experience than anything," I replied and then paused before continuing to speak. "I got a two-year degree, but I keep that to myself. It ain't really nothing to talk about in the hood. But what about you? In the car you was saying you in school. What's your major?"

"Nursing."

I nodded my head and drank some more sake. "That's a good look."

"You don't seem like the college type," Jasmine said to me. "No offense, I'm just saying."

"Quiet as it's kept, I never even finished high school. But I got my G.E.D. and then I went to community college because I always wanted more than just these streets, you feel me?"

Jasmine nodded her head yes.

"I own twelve Taco Bells, twelve Subway sandwich shops, and I also own twelve income tax franchises."

"Wow! That's really good. So you're a businessman."

"Entrepreneur."

"Oh, my bad." Jasmine laughed. "Why is everything that you own in groups of twelve? And why you still fuckin' with the streets if you sitting on all of that?"

I laughed. "You just passed exam number two."

"You better stop with all these goddamn tests," she joked.

Then I explained that I liked the fact that she paid attention to details and told her how important that was in life. I went on to explain to her that in the Bible certain numbers had significance, and that the number twelve represented completion and perfection, so that's why I did things in groups of twelve.

"Interesting. So you're a smart businessman that knows the Bible and could teach me a lot about life. Always the good ones that are taken. *Dayum!*" She laughed. "So when are you getting married?"

"We set the date for next New Year's Eve."

"Oh, OK. A New Year's Eve wedding. That's different," Jasmine said and then she paused before continuing to talk. "Let me ask you something."

"Yeah. What's up?"

"Mia don't ever encourage you to leave the streets alone?"

I shook my head no, and looked at Jasmine to see where she was going with her words.

"If I was your girl, I woulda switched up my major and gone for my MBA or something business-related. On the real, you got all those franchises and all that. All you need is somebody to help you take that to a billion-dollar level. I remember seeing this fat black guy on BET and he owns like five hundred Burger Kings. And he had his own custom made G5 and the whole nine. With the right woman in your corner, that could easily be you."

I nodded my head and just listened.

After our food arrived, I ordered more sake for us because we had finished the first round that quick. But it was a good thing, because the sake had us both feeling pretty good, and I wanted to keep it flowing.

"You gonna get me drunk up in here, and it's only two in the afternoon," Jasmine said.

"It's nighttime somewhere in the world."

Jasmine laughed, and then she adjusted herself in her seat before digging into her food. That was when I decided to place my hand on her right thigh underneath the table. I gently massaged and stroked her thigh, until I got to her knee, and then I massaged that part of her body.

"You better focus on your food and not me, 'cause you ain't ready for this," Jasmine said.

I laughed and I removed my hand from her leg. Ten minutes later I went back to flirting with her.

"So I ain't ready for you, huh?"

Jasmine wagged her index finger from side to side as she finished chewing her shrimp. "See, I didn't say that. Remember what you just told me about the importance of paying attention to detail. What I said was you ain't ready for *this*."

Jasmine was real quick with it and witty, and I liked that. What I liked even better was what she was implying.

"That's what you think?"

"That's what I know," she added, and then she drank some more sake.

"That's that South Side swagger talking. But, remember, I'm from Brooklyn, so you know how we get down. But I like your confidence."

"I got reason to be confident, but it ain't got nothing to do with the South Side."

"So where does the confidence come from?"

"I'm just saying. Just how you got some dudes and they know what they workin' with, the same is true for some women. And I know what I'm workin' with. My pussy is nice and fat and juicy." Jasmine smiled and paused for effect. "And like I said, you ain't ready for this."

The sake was definitely having its effect on me, and with Jasmine talking about her pussy, I was ready to take her back to my crib, which wasn't too far from the restaurant, and fuck her brains out. But I decided to just keep myself in check and play things cool for the moment.

I placed my hand back on Jasmine's thigh. Only this time I didn't focus on her knee. Instead I worked my hand upward until I got to her crotch area and I started to rub on her pussy.

She immediately stopped me though. "When you really ready for this, let me know and we'll revisit that then. I don't think your Mia would be too happy right now."

I nodded my head and I played things cool and kept everything in line with the way things had been flowing.

"You just passed your final exam," I said to Jasmine.

She smirked and looked at me and then went back to eating her food.

Before long we had finished eating and we made it back to my car. I had the driver swing by my house, which wasn't too far from the restaurant. I knew that Mia wouldn't be there because ever since the break in she had felt more comfortable staying at my apartment in Manhattan and that's where she was at the moment.

I lived in Kings Point, a very exclusive area in Long Island. Jasmine had never been to that part of Long Island. I genuinely had to stop back at my crib and pay the contractor that was doing some work at my house. Since I was heading to Manhattan after dropping off Jasmine in Queens, it made sense to just swing by the crib and knock it out at that point.

When we reached my crib I exited the car, but Jasmine stayed put. I ran inside and paid the contractor, and shortly thereafter, I was back at the car.

"Come inside," I said to Jasmine and extended my hand to her.

"Nico, where's Mia?" Jasmine said in a loud whisper, a devilish grin on her face.

"We good. Don't worry about that. She's in the city."

Jasmine shook her head, looking at me while she exited the car. "I cannot believe you."

I led Jasmine into my crib and didn't waste time taking her on a tour or any of that because the truth of the matter was, I just wanted to bang her out real quick and be in and out, since Mia was waiting on me in the city to take her to lunch at Ciprani.

Jasmine followed behind me as I walked and asked me if she could use the bathroom. So I took her coat from her and showed her where the bathroom was, and I went into the guest bedroom right next to my master bedroom and hung up both of our coats and waited for her to finish using the bathroom.

When she was done, she exited the bathroom and looked around to see where I had gone.

"I'm in here," I said to Jasmine, and she walked over to me.

I closed the door behind her and locked it, and then I pulled her close to me.

"Nico, you're buggin'!" Jasmine said, trying to push me away from her. "We can't do nothin' in here."

I continued to lean in, trying to kiss her until she gave in. She pressed her lips against mine, and I slid my tongue into her mouth and started to kiss her. Jasmine held on to me tightly and kissed me harder than I kissed her. I could feel her chest heaving in and out.

"OK, wait, wait, wait." Jasmine quickly pulled away from me and fanned herself with both of her hands. She looked at me and told me we couldn't do anything in my house.

I pulled her back close to me and turned her so that her back was to my chest, and unbuttoned her jeans.

"You was talking that shit—Let me see how fat that pussy is." I kissed her on her neck. Then I slid my hand into her jeans and started to play with her clit.

"How did this happen? We just met," Jasmine said, sounding real faint, her eyes closed.

Her pussy was soaked, so I knew she was enjoying the way I was making her feel. I slid my middle finger inside her pussy and started to finger-fuck her.

"Oh my God! You are driving me insane," Jasmine said to me while I continued to kiss on her neck. She then reached back and started to feel on my rock-hard dick. "I wantchu," she said, her eyes closed. She unzipped my pants and reached her hand in and grabbed hold of my dick.

I took off my shirt, and Jasmine turned around and touched my chest and my six-pack and looked at my tats. I took off my boots, and Jasmine took off hers as well. She also took off her jeans, revealing a pair of purple thongs. Just looking at her body made me feel like I was going to nut right there on the spot. Jasmine then took off her shirt, but she left on her matching purple bra, and I took off my pants and my boxers.

Without me having to say anything, Jasmine came close to me and gave me a soft peck on the lips. She looked up at me, and I looked at her, and then she slowly bent down until her face was right in front of my dick. She started sucking on it, simultaneously stroking it with her right hand.

Just as I was getting into the blowjob, Jasmine stopped and looked up at me. She smiled as if she knew she was teasing me. I gently grabbed the back of her head and guided it back on to my dick, and she continued to suck on it like she was an experienced porn star.

And again, just as I was getting into it, she purposely stopped and looked up at me while she continued to stroke the head of my dick with her hand.

"Don't start nothing you can't finish," I said to her.

Jasmine held her left index finger to her mouth, indicating that she wanted me to be silent. Then he pushed my hard dick so that it was standing straight up against my stomach, and she started to gently suck on my balls while she stroked my dick.

I couldn't believe how good her tongue felt. "Ohhh shit!"

"I told you to be quiet." Jasmine smiled.

All I could do was direct her head back to my balls, and she continued to suck on them. Jasmine then turned her head in a way where her head was underneath my balls and she took her tongue and started to lick the area in between my balls and my asshole all the while stroking my dick. That shit felt so good, I had to stop her because I was going to bust in two minutes.

I guided Jasmine up to her feet and she looked at me and smiled because she knew she had perfect dick-sucking skills.

"Take off that thong," I said to her.

She slipped out of the thong and laid down on the bed, her legs spread apart, and she started to play with her pussy. "Is it fat enough for you?" she asked seductively.

I was so ready to run up in her raw, but I knew Shabazz had been fucking everything that moved, so I played it safe and I went into my pants pocket and took out a Magnum and slid it on my dick. I told Jasmine to turn around.

Jasmine turned around so that her ass was facing me, on her hands and knees, while her feet dangled off the edge of the bed.

I slowly slid my dick into her pussy, and she gasped when my dick first went it inside her. Her pussy was tight like a virgin's. After a few gentle strokes to get things started, I was fucking her as hard as I could.

I did my best to bang Jasmine's back out, but she was taking all of my dick like a trooper. She put her face into the bed so that her ass was fully up in the air and accessible. As I wore her pussy out, she reached and grabbed a pillow and buried her face in it to muffle her screams and moans.

After about five minutes she moved the pillow from her face, and she turned and looked at me. "You making sure I remember that dick!" she said. "Emmmmhhh! You feel so good inside me!"

At this point I could tell that all of Jasmine's reservations were gone. She asked me if she could turn over on her back, so I let her, and then I continued to fuck her missionary style.

"You gonna make me come like this," she said to me.

I started to fuck her harder.

"Yeah, baby!" she screamed. "Give me that dick!"

I kept fucking her, and thirty seconds later, she was coming. She wrapped her legs around me and pulled me all the way into her and grabbed my ass with both of her hands. She was coming so hard, she didn't even realize she was scratching the shit out of me in the process.

When she was done coming, she looked up at me, breathing heavily. She playfully slapped me. "I hate your black ass! I don't even know how the hell this happened!" she said through a smile.

I paid her no mind and kept fucking her, and two minutes later I came. The shit felt so good, I didn't even pull my dick out of her pussy. I was just hoping the condom didn't break or anything, and thankfully it didn't.

"Look at you sweating like crazy." Jasmine wiped some sweat from my forehead and smiled at me. She covered her face and shook her head.

"What?"

"Now I don't wanna leave," she said.

I stood up and took off the condom, and Jasmine sat up.

"I don't wanna leave either." I gently touched her face and gave her a peck on the lips. "We gonna get together again when we got more time for each other."

We both began to get dressed before making our way out of the house and to my car, where my driver was waiting for us.

As we headed back to Queens, Jasmine was pretty much quiet for most of the ride. I was surprised she hadn't even at least commented on my house, but there was no way in the world she wasn't impressed by it, especially considering where she was living in the hood.

When we reached the Liberty Avenue exit on the Van Wyck Expressway, I reached in my pocket, took out five hundred dollars, and handed it to Jasmine.

She gave me a confused look. "What's that for?"

"A small birthday present."

"Awww, thank you!" Jasmine said as she took hold of the money. "That's so sweet." She leaned over and kissed me on the cheek.

Before long we had pulled into the front of Jasmine's house. I told the driver to give us a minute. Then I held out my hand to Jasmine and she placed her hand inside of mine.

"So we finally got to link up," I said.

Jasmine grinned from ear to ear. "Yes, we *definitely* did."

There were no other words to be said at that point, so I leaned into Jasmine's direction and kissed her on the lips. She didn't pull away from me. When I looked at her, her eyes were closed, so I took that as a green light and placed my hand on the back of her neck and started to tongue-kiss her. We kissed for about thirty seconds, and then I pulled away from her.

"You wasn't lying—Your shit is fat and juicy for real." I playfully tapped her on her chin with my hand.

"I never lie on myself."

She didn't wait for me to signal my driver to open the door. She unlocked her door and opened it, and as she was about to step out of the car, she thanked me for everything.

"Don't start running from me now," Jasmine said before fully exiting the car.

"We good. I gotchu. Keep my shit tight, ya heard?"

She looked at me and smiled, and nodding her head before closing the door.

I smiled to myself after watching her make it inside her house. I couldn't wait to fuck her again. Jasmine had good-ass pussy and good head, but that was just a side note as far as I was concerned. She didn't know it yet, but there was no way I was going to start running from her. I couldn't run from her if I wanted to, at least not until I got her to set up her man for me.

I was supposed to meet Mia for lunch in Manhattan, but I wasn't in the mood for her shit, so I called her and told her I couldn't make it. Instead I told my driver to take me to Harlem, so I could link up with BJ. I needed him and Lo on a flight like yesterday to link up with the Haitians out in Miami.

It was nearly three o'clock in the morning, and I could hear my cell phone vibrating from across the room. Mia stirred in bed, pretending to be asleep. I walked across our massive bedroom and grabbed my phone, thinking that it was Jasmine. To my shock, Bebo was blowing me up.

"Yo," I said.

"Yo, Nico, what took you so long to answer your phone?" Bebo asked, aggressively.

"I was 'sleep, muthafucka. Fuck you think took me so long?"

Bebo paused momentarily, "I need you, my nigga."

"A'ight, we'll politick in the morning."

"Nah, this can't wait. I can't talk this shit through the wire. Those peoples might be listening."

I exhaled as my mind raced on what to do. "So what you thinkin'?"

"Come through to the underground. I'm already here waitin' on you."

The underground was code for a basement stash house that we used for business meetings and other illegal shit. The apartment building was off of Hillside Avenue and 179th Street in Jamaica, Queens, where we would pay the super of the building a few grand a month. My gut told me something wasn't right—that this could be a setup. I could count on two hands the number of niggas I knew who left their cribs in the middle of the night to never come back. When Mia saw me getting dressed she began to panic.

"Who you going to meet?"

"I got shit to take care of."

"This late?"

"Go back to sleep. This shouldn't take long."

When she saw me reaching for my Glock, I could almost see her eyes relax, and I wasn't sure if I liked that. When she thought I was going to meet some bitch she was all worried and ready to beef. The moment she saw me reaching for my burner she was content with a nigga going out in the streets to possibly put my murder game down.

As soon as I got in my truck, I called BJ.

"Yo, did you get a call from Bebo?"

"Nah, why, what's good?"

"That nigga just called and asked me to meet him at the underground."

"This time of night?"

"Exactly."

"You want me to come through?"

"No doubt. And go by and pick up Lo. I don't trust Bebo. This might be an ambush, and I want to be on point. I don't want to walk in outnumbered and outgunned."

When I pulled up on the block I didn't see BJ and Lo, so I circled the block a few times just to see if I could spot anyone creeping. The block was desolate and quiet other than a few livery cabs driving down every few minutes. I was just about to hit BJ on his jack when he hit me.

"I see you," BJ stated. "We're parked down by the bodega. Come down and pick us up."

My eyes scanned the block and BJ flickered his high-beam lights. As my car crept up the block, I kept wondering what the fuck was so urgent to pull me out of my bed. When BJ and Lo got in my car they were wondering the exact same thing.

"Yo, this don't feel right," BJ stated the obvious. "That nigga didn't give you a hint as to what was up?"

I shook my head and tried to remain focused. "If y'all even feel like shit ain't right, just start blazing."

When we got downstairs to the lower level we heard a few hushed voices. Finally, Bebo called out, "Yo, Nico, that's you?"

"All day," I replied as I bent the corner. *Look at this dumb muthafucka,* I thought. With his mouth and hands duct-taped behind his back, battered and bruised sat Brandon. He was real fucked up. And surrounding him was Bebo, Corey, and Earl. When Brandon fucked up the hit on Skeen by allowing Shabazz to get away, I told him that he had to lay low until the dust settled. He sure had enough paper from the hit to get outta Dodge. As soon as our eyes met, I knew what time it was. He'd given me up.

"What's good?" I asked Bebo as if he didn't have a prisoner just inches from my face.

"I didn't know we was having a house party," Bebo remarked dryly. "Why don't we film this shit and put it up on YouTube?"

I smirked. "What are you talkin' 'bout?"

"You actin' brand new, Nico. I called *you* out. No disrespect, but why you bring your bodyguards."

"These are our soldiers, man. They'd take a bullet for you!" I stated, trying to feel out the situation. "You coulda been hemmed up in here for all I know, and if that were true, you woulda been happy to see these muthafuckas."

I wanted to mention that he had Corey and Earl flanked at his side, but that wasn't really the point.

Ignoring my last remark, Bebo walked over to Brandon and ripped his duct-tape from off his mouth.

"Listen to what this muthafucka is saying 'bout why he killed Skeen."

There wasn't anything that Brandon could say that I didn't already know. I took out my Glock and emptied three joints into his chest cavity. No need in prolonging the inevitable. There wasn't any way that he was walking out of there alive and on the strength of his sister—an ex girlfriend of mine—I put him out of his misery.

"Damn, Nico, why the fuck you do that?!" Bebo barked. His pressure had risen because he didn't get the show he wanted. He wanted to see the look on my face when Brandon said that I'd paid him to murder Skeen.

"It don't matter why he murdered Skeen. Y'all niggas shoulda handled this already. I don't know why you sittin' here babysitting this muthafucka!"

BJ wasn't a dummy. He chimed in to help bolster my action. "Y'all know Nico is quick to let his thang go! If you wanted someone more diplomatic, then you called the wrong dude."

I nodded my head in agreement as Bebo glared at me. I continued to grip the handle of my Glock, never tucking it back in my waist. If Corey or Earl even flinched, I'd body them both.

After a few tense seconds, I stated. "Yo, we out. I got outta my bed for this?"

"Oh, no doubt," Bebo replied. He switched up his mood and body language quickly. "But, yo, what about the work? We still gonna fuck with the niggas from the party? I need you to come through tomorrow for a meeting with them."

"Just let me know the time and place and I'll be there," I said. "How much work we talkin'?"

"Between seventy and eighty keys a month of that pure Columbian uncut shit. Straight off the boat."

I nodded.

"A'ight, tomorrow. Hit me up."

As we walked toward my car BJ asked in a rushed whisper, "We not fucking with that snitch are we?"

"Hell nah! And I ain't going to no meeting that the feds will be listening in on. Fuck that! Bebo has got to go, but we gotta do it right.

He has to disappear and never be found." I leaned on my car. "BJ, I'm putting you on that. Get rid of that muthafucka!"

CHAPTER 12

Mia

Ever since I suspected that Jasmine might have something going on with Nico, it was almost like I had become obsessed with knowing who Nico was with and what he was doing every second of the day.

I had never spoken up and confronted him about Jasmine because I was afraid of what his reaction might be. Plus, other than the fact that they were calling and texting each other, it wasn't like I had any other hardcore proof that they were actually fucking.

One thing I did was, I started keeping tabs on every number that showed up on Nico's phone bill just to see if I saw any kind of patterns. Whenever I saw a number on his bill that I didn't recognize, I would block my phone number and call that number to see who picked up. And I would also Google the phone number just to see what would come up.

Nico was staying in contact with a chick in Maryland on a regular basis. I had a good idea who she was, but I wasn't one hundred percent sure. And there was also another chick with a Virginia phone number he was calling on a regular basis, but I had no idea who she was.

Seeing that those two chicks were out of town, I didn't really look at them as too much of a threat, compared to Jasmine, who was right here in New York with Nico and had daily access to him.

Jasmine was not respecting me at all, in terms of contacting Nico. From the pattern of her calls and texts to him, I could see clearly that something was up because the calls and texts were all throughout the day and night. And it was starting to increase to the point where she was in contact with him more than I was.

I made sure I called everybody I knew who lived in Queens and asked them did they know who Jasmine was. It proved to be a small world, because a few people I was cool with either knew her personally, or knew of her through other people. I made sure I took mental notes on everything people were telling me about her.

I kept hearing how cool Jasmine was with some chick named Simone, and I kept hearing how she was quickly trying to become the next big video vixen. The other thing I kept hearing was that Jasmine and her crew were nothing but money-hungry, gold-digging ghetto whores.

Basically, after doing my informal background check on Jasmine, I didn't feel like she was the absolute biggest threat in the world. But, regardless, she was still a threat, and I wanted her removed from the picture, so I kept digging and investigating to see what else I could find out.

What turned out to be a wild revelation to me was, on the same day I had called Jasmine and told her to stop calling Nico, I noticed an incoming phone number on his account history. It looked like the call went to voice mail, because it was only one minute long. So I blocked my number and called it back, and the call ended up going to voice mail. There was a female's voice on the voice mail, but

I wasn't sure who the chick was. The fact that the number had a New York area code definitely piqued my interest, though, so I Googled it.

I was shocked by what I saw come up in Google. There was a long list of links from Google that took me to Craigslist ads associated with the number, all in the escort section of Craigslist. I clicked on all of the ads I saw in Google, and each ad had some chick named Chyna who was basically prostituting herself, but she wasn't making it blatant. For example, one ad said she was offering "full service for two hundred and fifty roses," and other similar ads had different prices, but they were all obvious cover-ups for prostitution.

Immediately after seeing all of those ads, my heart started to beat with fear. I was wondering if Nico was paying for pussy, and if he was, how long had he been doing this? And with how many chicks? Why would he feel the need to fuck prostitutes?

My heart continued to pound as I looked at the ads. I was trying my hardest to see if I could recognize who the chick was. It was hard to tell for sure because, in some of the pictures, her face was blurred out, and in other pictures, she had a black line passing through the upper part of her face. In some pictures you could tell that she took a picture of herself with her back facing a mirror so that you couldn't see her face, and you could only see her ass and the back of her body in the picture.

I analyzed every picture. All of a sudden it was like my heart stopped, and I realized that Chyna could actually have been Jasmine. "Oh my fuckin' God!" I said out loud to myself.

Immediately I called the number back from my blocked number, and again the phone rang out to voice mail. I listened really closely to see if could make out the person's voice, but I wasn't able to say for sure that it was Jasmine.

I went back to looking at the pictures, and before I knew it, more than an hour had passed by, and I was still analyzing them. I was becoming more and more convinced that it was, in fact, Jasmine in the pictures. The girl in the pictures was the same complexion as Jasmine, and looked to be about the same height, and had the same hair color and hair texture.

Finally after playing detective for what seemed like hours, I saw part of a tattoo on the back of the girl's right hand, only partially exposed. I went back and looked at all of the ads again, and in each ad, the tattoo was not visible. I realized that it was purposely covered up.

"That's muthafuckin' Jasmine!" I said out loud to myself after looking at the picture with the partial tattoo again. I was one hundred and fifty percent certain that Jasmine had a tattoo on her right hand. So then I sat there and connected all of the dots in my own mind. There was no way this could all be coincidence.

Like, what were the chances that both Jasmine and some other random chick would both have tattoos on their right hand and they both called Nico?

"You fucking bitch! I'm about to blow up your whole shit!" I said out loud to myself. I was ready to go to war like I was a chick from the hood.

I started to print out each ad that I saw, just in case they somehow got deleted or I couldn't find them again at a later date.

At that point my heart wasn't beating as fast, and I was feeling confident because I now knew exactly how to pull Jasmine's card. I grabbed my cell phone and was going to call her, but instead I decided to send her a text message.

You couldn't just stay in your own fucking lane! You had to test me. It's all good because I'm about to pull your card!!! ☺

No more than two minutes after I sent that text, Jasmine texted me right back and said:

I could tell you some Real hurtful shit but I won't. Keep fucking annoying me though and I just might.

I laughed when I read her message because I couldn't wait to see what Jasmine's response would be to my next text message to her which was:

Whateva bitch! Don't make me tell the world your nickname...

After I sent that text message, I waited and I waited, and after about an hour I realized that Jasmine wasn't going to respond to me. I thought that she was probably panicking and freaking out, wondering if I knew that her prostitution nickname was Chyna.

I decided to send her another text just to get under her skin.

Don't say I didn't warn you not to fuck with my MAN!!!

Once again, after I sent that text, I got no response from her. I knew I had touched the right nerve. I wasn't satisfied though with just knowing that Chyna was out there prostituting herself. I wanted to see if I could find out anything more about her best friend Simone and also this dude name Carlos, who was supposedly her manager for her music video career.

CHAPTER 13

Jasmine

By the time I was done smoking, I was feeling nice. Weed always put me in a talkative I-don't-give-a-fuck mode. And at that point I didn't give a fuck that it was almost two in the morning. I took out my phone and searched for Nico's number. When I found it, I decided to block my number before calling him, just in case he was with Mia and her crazy ass. I didn't want to blow up his spot and make myself look bad in his eyes.

The phone rang twice, and then Nico picked up.

"Hey, Nico. This is Jasmine. Can you talk?"

"Yeah, I can. What's up? You OK?"

"I'm good. But I just wanna be straight up with you about something."

"What's up?" Nico asked.

"I don't know how to say it, but you just really made this impression on me, and I don't know how to shake it."

Nico laughed. "Is that right?"

"Yeah, that's right. I know it's late, but I just wanted to call you and tell you that. I wanted to text you something, but I didn't wanna just send you a text without calling you first. So can I hang up and then text you something?"

"Yeah, it's all good."

"OK." I was preparing to end the call, but Nico said happy birthday to me before I could hang up. I paused for a moment.

"Your birthday is Saturday, right?" he asked, breaking the silence.

"Yeah, it is."

"Well, it's after midnight, so technically it's Saturday."

"No, I get it. I'm just surprised that you remembered that."

"I pay attention to details," Nico reminded me.

I laughed and then I told him that I would text him in a few minutes, and we both hung up the phone.

I took a quick five-minute shower. I lathered up my ass, and before rinsing it off, I opened the shower door and grabbed my phone and snapped a picture of my soapy ass. I put the phone back down and finished taking my shower.

After drying off, I put baby oil all over my body. With my phone I took a close-up picture of my clean, glistening pussy. Then I spread open my pussy lips and took another picture. I saved all three pictures to my phone, and then I opened up all three of the pictures to examine them, to make sure they all looked good, before sending them to Nico with a message that read:

I hope you like what you see. It's all yours. You can have it whenever you want. -xoxoxo.

In a way I was kind of hoping that Mia did see those pictures of my ass and my pussy that I sent to Nico. Although I didn't know exactly what Mia was referring to when she had sent me that text message about her telling the world my nickname, I hadn't heard from her since that day and I didn't want her to think that she had backed me down or somehow scared me off with punk-ass threats.

After sending the text to Nico, I looked at my phone and saw that I had multiple missed calls from my crew that I was supposed to link up with at B.B. King's. I also had two missed calls from Shabazz and a text message from him asking me to call. I really didn't want to call him back because I was so open off Nico. But if I did, perhaps I could get some information that I could relay to Nico and score some brownie points.

Just as I was about to call Shabazz, I looked at my phone and saw it was Nico texting me back.

I want some more of that.

I immediately hit him back. *Then let's make it happen for my birthday.*

Nico texted me right back. *Done deal.*

Next, I called Shabazz and he asked me to meet him near the Belt Parkway at the Mobil gas station off of Springfield Boulevard. When I got there, I parked. And waited. After waiting about thirty minutes and calling him relentlessly, I was just about to leave when he walked up and tapped my window.

"Damn, Shabazz, you scared the shit out of me!"

"Leave the car here and follow me." His voice was gruff and his eyes were shifty, darting around the area.

"I'm not leaving my father's car here. It'll get towed."

"Leave the shit here!" he commanded. "My man inside will watch it. I know the owner."

I grabbed my pocketbook and followed Shabazz. We walked through the Mobil station toward the restricted employee area. In the back there were several surveillance cameras and an Indian guy keeping close watch. I scanned the room and saw a massive safe and two coffee cups. Shabazz grabbed his NY fitted baseball cap. Immediately, I copped an attitude.

"You been sitting in here watching me all this time?"

Ignoring my question, he addressed his friend. "Yo, Hassuan, I'm out. I'll hit you on your jack in the morning."

"And make sure you watch my father's car!" I ordered.

Hassuan smiled slightly but didn't reply. Shabazz led me out a back entrance and we jumped into his truck. As soon as he started the ignition he leaned over and gave me a quick peck on my lips.

"I missed you," he said softly.

I rolled my eyes. "Then why haven't you been checkin' for me? You don't answer my calls and just leave a bitch out here alone." I then added, "And broke."

"I got a lot of complicated shit to figure out, and I don't want you in harm's way. Shit could get thick. Believe me, the less you know the better. Your big-ass mouth could get you in a lot of trouble."

I turned the radio to 98.7 Kiss radio before beefing. "Since when do I got a big mouth?"

Shabazz chuckled. "Since you learned how to speak, I'm guessing." He pointed toward the back seat. "Yo, grab that bottle in the back and pour me a drink."

That was right up my alley. I leaned over and grabbed a brown paper bag. Shabazz had stopped at the liquor store and bought a bottle of Hennessy for himself and a bottle of Nuvo for me. Two plastic cups and four blunts were already rolled. I knew Shabazz had a drinking problem. But his problems were his problems. I just wanted to have a good time and possibly leave with a couple dollars in my pocket. Once the liquor was flowing I sparked up a blunt.

Finally, I asked. "Where we going?"

"New Jersey. I got a hotel room out there."

"We going to Atlantic City?"

"Nah, just chill," Shabazz replied. "And stop asking so many questions."

"Why you on some new shit? You used to be able to tell me everything, and now you're acting all weird and paranoid. I'm not in the mood for no crazy, 007 bullshit, Shabazz. So if you're gonna start actin' all loony tunes, you can turn this muthafuckin' truck right back around!"

Shabazz cut his eyes toward me and began to chuckle. "A'ight, I feel you. It's just that so much is at stake that I knew I had to bounce."

"OK, well tell me everything and maybe I can help you."

Shabazz held out his cup and waited for me to refill it. And then he continued, "It's about Skeen's murder. I keep replaying what happened over and over in my mind, and it's just not adding up. It's obvious that it was a setup—"

"Yeah, but shit like that happens all the time, right? Stickup kids runnin' up on drug dealers."

Shabazz cut to the chase. "It was Nico, Jasmine. I'm telling you that muthafuckin' bitch-ass nigga set us up to get killed, and I promise you I'm gonna splatter his fuckin' brains out on the hot pavement!"

Now I was hyped. "Nico? Why the fuck would he want you and Skeen murdered? Why would he put the wolves on his own people?"

"I don't know why!" Shabazz began to get really animated and the car began to accelerate. "All I know is that shit ain't adding up, and when shit don't add up you gotta go back to the basics."

"Slow down," I warned. "I'm not trying to spend the night locked up."

Shabazz eased his foot off the accelerator. "I'm telling you, the night Bebo came home he was acting real extra. He kept talking about the wolves and goons and shit like that."

"So?"

"So? It was all an act to me. Like he wanted to go overboard in showing Bebo that I'd fucked up to take the focus off of how I almost lost my life and that we'd been set up!"

"I think you reaching. Nico's concerned about you."

Shabazz was quiet for a long, uncomfortable moment. And then he spoke up, "Word, so what's up with that dude? You really think he's good peoples, like I could trust him?"

"I do, Shabazz. He seems genuinely concerned about you."

"You tell him you were meeting me tonight?"

"Why would I tell him that?" I laughed nervously. "I don't even know him like that."

"Right…right. And what about his girl, what's her name again?" Shabazz began to snap his fingers in a continual gesture.

"Mia."

"Yeah, Mia. I remember you said y'all were getting cool."

"I ain't cool with that crazy bitch!" I spat.

Suddenly, Shabazz gave me a backhanded slap that made me see stars. "You fuckin' that nigga ain't you?"

"Ain't noboby—"

The second hit was more of a punch, and the pain was magnified. I hunched over in my seat and cradled my head with my arms to block any further blows, but none came. We continued to drive for a few more minutes until I could feel the car slow down until we eventually came to a complete stop. My heart was palpitating from fear. Any high I'd previously felt from the liquid had dissipated, quickly. My senses were heightened and I'd do almost anything to be back home in the security of my own room.

Shabazz flung open my door and dragged me out by my hair.

"What are you doing!" I screamed. "I ain't fuckin' him!"

I looked around and we were in a deserted area. I could see the New Jersey Turnpike not too far in the distance.

"You're a dumb-ass trick! He only fucked you to get at me, but you're too stupid to see that!"

Shabazz tossed me on the ground and began stomping me in my stomach and gut. The pain was excruciating, but I knew that he could do much worse. I continued to deny that I'd slept with Nico, but Shabazz knew the truth. Finally he demanded, "Take off your clothes."

"Shabazz, come on now. You've done enough. Just take me home!" I tried to sound authoritative, but he wasn't listening. He had a wild look in his eyes—a mixture of hurt, pain and anger.

From his waist he pulled out his burner. "That nigga tried to rock me to sleep and my girl goes and fucks him!" Shabazz hit the side of his head with his pistol like a mad man. "Do you know how that makes me feel? Huh, bitch?"

He was now towering over me in a menacing stance. "On my life I didn't fuck him! I wouldn't do something like that to you. I swear to God!"

"I said, strip!"

"Shabazz—"

Pop, pop, pop, pop, pop!

Shabazz let off a succession of shots around my immediate perimeter. "Strip! Whore! Don't make me ask you again!"

Reluctantly, I began to take off my clothes as my hands trembled. My tears and pleas didn't affect Shabazz at all. He kept his gun steadied on me until I was literally butt naked. He then scooped up my clothes, hopped in his truck, and peeled out.

For the first twenty minutes I foolishly thought he'd come back for me. After an hour, realization sank in.

CHAPTER 14

Nico

On the Saturday morning of Jasmine's birthday, I had gotten numerous calls from an unknown New Jersey number, and when I called it back it was a police precinct. I immediately hung up. I didn't have a clue who was calling me from a precinct, but it didn't sit too well with me.

The Haitian cartel I had connected BJ and Lo with came through. They had good product, and our organization was back up and running. That was a good look, but until I knocked off Bebo and Shabazz, I couldn't break out the celebratory champagne just yet. Their product cost two stacks more per key than my former Columbian connect, but I knew once we began moving enough volume that they'd be more competitive with their pricing. And they only guaranteed the shipment as far as North Carolina. Our mules had to take the risk from North Carolina to New York, which was another problem that I could negotiate at a later date. Bebo's alleged snitching was costing our organization money.

Ever since the impromptu meeting at the underground, Bebo had been on my ass. There was no way I was going to go with Bebo's bullshit-ass plan to partner with other crews so we could all eat off the same package. I kept brushing him off, giving him excuse after excuse as to why I couldn't link up and he was less than livid. His behavior was bordering on passive. Which if anyone *truly* knew Bebo, they would know he was a hothead. And doing a seven year bid didn't mellow him out. The reason he hadn't orchestrated a hit on not only me but Mia as well, was most likely because he was working for those peoples. The feds ain't down with giving any green light to an assassination. They wanted me, and our crew, doing football numbers. As each day went by, I was starting to really believe that Bebo was a snitch and the rumor was no longer that. It was a muthafuckin' hard fact.

When the late afternoon approached I got a call from a 718 area code with a Queens exchange. I ignored that too. I usually didn't get calls from unknown numbers because very few people had my cell phone number. But today, it was nonstop. I allowed it to go to voicemail and this time a message was left. When I listened to the message it was Jasmine telling me she was calling from her home number and not to call her cell phone because Shabazz had it. Immediately, my interest was piqued. I dialed her right away.

"Happy birthday!"

"Nico?" Jasmine replied.

"Who you just call?"

"Ahhh, thank you," she sang into the phone. "You're too sweet."

"Listen, what's up with Shabazz having your phone? You seen him?"

"I don't really want to talk about it . . ."

"Then why the fuck you mentioned him?" I snapped.

"Whoa, be easy," she began. "I only mentioned him when I left you the message because there's no telling what he'd do to me if he saw you calling my phone."

"Didn't I tell you to call me if he came around? How fuckin' hard was that to follow!"

She began to whine. "Baby—"

"Don't call me baby, Jasmine. I'm a grown-ass man! When the fuck did that nigga come through to take your phone?"

She exhaled and then there was silence.

"Answer me!" I barked. I was beyond playing with this broad. "That nigga Shabazz sent the hit squad up in my crib, and you're spewing baby talk!"

She cleared her throat and began to speak like a grown woman. "He came through last night on the humble after I had sent you a text. He scared the shit outta me. Then I remembered what you said and I tried to sneakily text you to let you know what was up. That's when he snatched my phone, saw the naked pictures, and bounced with my shit. He took my purse too..."

"So no doubt he done saw the naked pictures and all the texts that you already sent to me unless you deleted them all."

"I guess you're right."

"Then why are you calling me the next day asking me to not call or text you? The nigga already got everything he needs in your cellie."

"Yeah, but—"

"Yo, you knew our circumstances from jump. Why didn't you delete all that freak shit? What if he shows my girl?"

Jasmine's voice elevated. "I was trying to delete the messages and that's when he snatched my phone! He also took my pocketbook with my birthday money from my parents. He took my thousand dollars!"

"Word," I replied, unenthused. "I'll replace that, no doubt. But you gotta look out for me too."

"Anything," she purred, obviously thinking I was talking about sex. "Whatever your pleasure."

"Anything?" I repeated.

"Anything!" she assured.

"A'ight, just remember that."

Right after I hung up with Jasmine, my attorney called. He had gotten wind that the feds were working on a secret indictment that was going to be so wide-sweeping, it was probably going to take out my whole organization of underlings—the mules, corner boys, and trigger men. If convicted, everybody would be facing life sentences.

"What does this mean?" I asked.

"Well, technically, right now, not much that concerns you. These indictments are for low-level street dealers that are looking to cut a deal. If they cooperate there isn't much they could say regarding your dealings with them because you don't deal directly with them, which is good. But if they could get someone, anyone, in your organization on a higher chain of command, like your underboss—"

"Or partner."

"Exactly. Anyone with substance to turn states evidence then we got a problem. The feds would much rather incorporate the testimony of high-level people in Ghetto Mafia than runners who can't even pick you out in a lineup. If that should happen I'll do my best for you but you got to do your part too."

"Which is?"

"This is drop a hefty retainer over at my office as soon as possible. That way if you can't get to your funds, or your assets are frozen you won't have to worry about having a legal aid represent you against the federal government. I mean, I love you man but I can't support my family working for pro bono."

"OK, done. What else?"

"Nico, be very, very cautious on every move you make moving forward. Keep your hands as clean as possible if you know what I mean. And tie-up all loose ends."

I took heed to everything my attorney had to say. I took an hour to mediate on what moves I needed to make and then I redialed Jasmine.

"Yo, I booked a room at the Marriott Marquis in lower Manhattan. Meet me there and I'll bring you your dough. I want to celebrate your birthday. I miss you."

"Oh my god!" she squealed. "What made you change your tone with me?"

I blew some air into the phone, genuinely feeling pressure and stress. "Don't worry about all that. Be there by nine."

After we ended our phone call, I jumped in the shower and then drove myself to Manhattan in my Yukon Denali.

Just as I was pulling out of my driveway, Mia was pulling into the driveway in her Range Rover with her good friend Sharmel. I stopped the car and rolled down the window and spoke to them.

"Hey, baby," Mia said to me.

"What's up? What's good, Sharmel?"

"Hey Nico." Sharmel said.

"Where you heading?" Mia asked.

"Out."

Mia knew not to over question me on exactly where I was going.

"We still going to breakfast and to the spa in the morning?"

I looked at her in confusion.

"Nico! Remember, I booked everything for us a couple of weeks ago?" Mia said, sounding kind of annoyed.

"Oh yeah, yeah. I just drew a blank. I'll be back tonight kind of late, but we'll be good for tomorrow. What time we heading out?" I said, even though I had no idea what the hell Mia was referring to.

"Eight o'clock I want us to leave. OK?" she asked, looking for reassurance from me.

"A'ight, I'll be here. So I'm out. Sharmel, good seeing you," I said, rolling up my window and pulling off.

I reached the Marriot Marquis at about nine-fifteen. By the time I parked the car and made it up to the room, it was a little after nine-thirty. I knocked on the door of room 2209 and waited.

After about a minute or so, Jasmine unlocked the door and opened it. I can't front—She looked good as hell, and instantly my dick got hard. She was wearing an all-black crotchless fishnet body stocking along with a pair of black marabou slippers with a three-inch heel. A smile came across my face, and I walked in.

Jasmine closed the door behind me. "Shhhhh," she said to me. She put her index finger to her mouth and prevented me from saying anything.

After dimming the lights in the room, she took hold of my hand and led me from the foyer and into the room and stopped me right in front of the king-size bed. She started rubbing on my dick through my jeans, and tongue-kissing me. After about a minute of kissing, she unbuckled my belt and then unbuttoned the fly to my jeans and pulled out my hard dick. Before I could blink, she was on her knees and sucking my dick just like she had done in my crib. The only difference was, this time she was deep-throating my shit, and she wasn't using no hands.

I was speechless, enjoying everything.

While Jasmine sucked my dick, I took off my hat, my leather coat, my shirt, and my wife-beater. I massaged her soft hair while she pleased me with her tongue. Jasmine definitely had skills, and she knew how to suck dick better than women twice her age.

"Yeahhhh, make that shit nice and wet for me, baby," I instructed her.

Like a pro, Jasmine continued to please me, making sure not to use her hands.

"Ohhh shit! I love that right there."

Jasmine licked my balls with her tongue, while deep-throating my dick. My dick had literally disappeared in her mouth, and her lips were touching my balls. Then, somehow, with my dick literally touching her tonsils, she managed to slide her tongue out and was licking my balls with her tongue.

I had fucked many bad-ass dime pieces, hood rats and everything in between, and hands down, by far, Jasmine was giving me the best blowjob I'd ever had.

Ten minutes into the blowjob, Jasmine wasn't showing any signs of slowing down or quitting or even getting tired. Most chicks would have been complaining of lockjaw or saying that they were tired or something like that by that time. But not Jasmine. She was a certified pro, and she was going hard.

To encourage her, I grabbed the back of her head and guided her in rhythm back and forth on my dick. It felt like an instant replay of the last time she had sucked my dick.

I let go of Jasmine's head and told her I was about to come.

Finally she spoke her first words since opening the door for me. "I want you to come in my mouth." She stuck out her tongue and waited for me to shoot my load.

When I came, my sperm shot everywhere. Some of it got in Jasmine's hair, some of it landed on her neck, her cheek, her collarbone, and a lot of it landed right on her tongue and she swallowed it like it was jelly.

Jasmine then smiled. She looked up at me and watched my reaction. "I like this big vein on your dick." She giggled before getting up off her knees. She stood up and went to the bathroom and came back real quick. She must have gone to the bathroom to clean herself off, because when she came back all of the come was out of her hair and off the rest of her body.

Jasmine lay down on the king-size bed, her legs open, and tapped on her pussy with her right hand. Again, this was like *déjà vu*, because things were so reminiscent of how they had been in my crib.

"My turn," she said.

"Your turn?"

"Yup. I mean it is *my* birthday. I want you to eat me."

It was at that moment I realized a slight bruise on the left side of her face, no doubt from Shabazz. Something had gone down in the wee hours of the morning, but whatever happened, I doubted I'd get the true story.

I slipped out of my boots, took off my jeans, and climbed onto the bed. I went face first into Jasmine's pussy. I rubbed on her spot and slipped my middle finger inside of her, and she moaned, closing her eyes and rotating her hips in pleasure.

"Look at this clit."

"You like it?"

"I love it! It's fuckin' fat as hell!"

"I was trying to tell you."

I sucked on her clit and simultaneously worked my finger in her pussy, forcefully massaging her G-spot.

"Oh my God! Nico, you gonna make me come!" Jasmine was working her hips and grinding her pussy into my tongue faster and faster. Then she grabbed hold of the back of my head and forced me to stay right where I was at.

I could tell she was about to come because it was like all of the muscles in her body got tense, and she got this crazy Incredible Hulk kind of strength, wrapping her legs around me and squeezing on my body tight as hell.

"Ahhhhhhhhhhhh!" she screamed as her body trembled and convulsed.

The next thing I knew, her pussy released juices all over my hand.

"Oh shit! Oh my God!" Jasmine said, breathing real heavy.

I laughed. "You actin' all crazy and I ain't even hit you with my dick yet."

"I'm sorry." Jasmine seemed kind of embarrassed, and she grabbed a pillow and covered her face.

By this time my dick was hard again. I reached in my jeans pocket for a condom. Jasmine still had her face covered, acting shy, but I knew there wasn't a shy bone in her body. I scooped her up by her hips and placed her so that her ass was at the edge of the bed, her back still on the bed. I spread her legs apart and pushed them back until the front of her thighs were touching the bed, and then I slid my dick inside her pussy, causing her to gasp.

I fucked her slow in the beginning. I knew women didn't like when dudes served up weak dick, so I had every intention of murdering her pussy just like I had done before.

Jasmine was flexible and limber, so she wasn't bothered at all when I repositioned her legs and pinned her feet behind her head and started fucking her as hard as I could. She was screaming, but I knew she was enjoying every stroke.

"Yessss! That's that grown-man dick right there!"

"You like the way I beat this pussy?"

"I love it! Murder that shit!"

Jasmine didn't have to cheer me on because my only goal was to leave her shit in cardiac arrest. Every stroke I delivered was so deep, I had to be hitting her kidneys or some shit. But to her credit she was a trooper, taking every stroke and enjoying it.

After about five minutes, Jasmine grabbed both of my butt cheeks, forcing me to fuck her even harder. She started to shake her head from side to side, and she closed her eyes. After she finished twitching, I turned her over and started fucking her doggy-style.

She turned and said to me, "You know you ain't right!"

I didn't bother to answer her because I was too focused on coming a second time myself. I clasped both of my hands behind my head and watched her ass giggle as I pumped my dick in and out of her pussy. Before long, I was coming a second time, and that nut felt better than the first one.

After I came, I beat on my chest like I was a gorilla.

"Told you I was gonna demolish that shit." I smacked her on her ass. "Happy birthday."

Jasmine looked at me seductively and she smiled. She then pulled back the covers on the bed and got under the sheets.

"Nah. You gotta give me my props, though 'cause I put it on you too."

"Yeah, but I won."

"You ain't win shit," she jokingly said. "If anything, that was a draw."

I laughed. "OK, I'll give you that. You won round one, but I won round two. So, yeah, it's a draw." Jasmine pulled the covers up to her neck and told me that she was tired and was going to take a nap.

I told her I was going to get dressed and then go downstairs to the View lounge and have some drinks, and that I would be back.

"OK, we gotta have a rematch later," she stated.

I laughed. I really liked her style a whole lot. She had good head and good pussy, and she seemed like she genuinely loved sex as much as a guy, so she had a lot going in her favor. But I still had to make sure I wasn't more focused on her pussy than I was on my business.

I came back up to the room Jasmine was asleep. I stripped naked and crawled into the bed next to her. She stirred in bed, realized I had returned, and then rubbed on my chest.

"Your body feels so good," she whispered. "It's so strong."

I wasn't one for pillow talk, but on this night I decided to engage in it because it gave me the perfect opportunity.

"You trust me?" I asked Jasmine.

The room was pretty dark, the only light peering into the room coming from the neon Times Square street lights and billboards twenty-two floors below our room. But even in the dark room I could see Jasmine look at me.

"Do I trust you? Of course, I do. Why?"

"I don't know what it is about you, but it's just this chemistry thing or something that I'm just really feeling. But you know my situation with Mia, and I don't wanna fuck that up and then find out that your ass wasn't really real. What I really should be asking you is do you love me."

Jasmine reached up and kissed me on my cheek. "You can trust me, baby. I don't have nothing to hide, and I don't have no agenda or none of that. And, as far as your situation goes with Mia, I'm a big girl. I knew what it was from the jump, but most importantly I do love you."

"So what's the deal with you and Shabazz?"

Jasmine responded quickly, "I hate him," a sound of disgust in her voice. She continued to rub on the left side of my stomach, her face on the left half of my chest.

"You said you trust me, right?"

"Yeah, I do," Jasmine replied. "Why you keep asking me that?"

"I'm asking you because I want you to do something for me, but I need to know that you trust me and that we're on the same page."

"OK, what's up?" Jasmine asked.

"I want you to murder Shabazz for me."

"What?" Jasmine said as she sat up.

"You heard what I asked you."

"Whoa. I was not expecting that at all."

Jasmine looked at me, I think, to determine if I was serious or if I was just testing her. And I kept quiet.

"You serious, aren't you?" she asked me.

I nodded my head.

Jasmine sat fully up and then she got out of the bed and walked to the other side of the room. She reached in her bag and got a blunt, and she asked me, "Do you mind if I smoke this blunt?"

"Nah, not at all. Do you. No judging, ever, from me," I declared. "I wouldn't ask you to do this if I wasn't down for you. You do this for me, and I got you on whatever it is you want."

I got up and held her. I could literally feel her heart beating a mile a minute.

Jasmine lit the blunt and, as she started to smoke, walked closer to the window. I followed her, and we both looked out onto the bright lights and the rich New York City skyline.

"Why though?" she asked me. "Why me?"

"Because I want you, and I gotta know that I can trust you, no matter what. And if I'm gonna keep it real, I just got word that an indictment is about to come down on me, and if they get Shabazz to talk, then I'm done. Everything I built is done, and me and my whole crew will be doing football numbers in prison."

Jasmine was quiet, and I kept quiet as she smoked her weed.

"But how you know for sure that he's snitching?"

"That's what I pay my lawyer and his investigators this big money. They find the shit out for me." I walked over and grabbed my phone, and then I came back over to her. "This is how good they are. One of the investigators took this." I handed her my phone for her to look at the picture I had just opened up.

"Oh my God! When was this?"

I had just showed her a picture of Shabazz fucking some chick in his truck. The picture was old, and Shabazz had sent it around to his boys a while ago bragging because he'd fucked a rival drug dealer's chick.

"I'm just saying; trust what I'm telling you. This nigga ain't never been down for you or for nobody else. He only been down for self, and he gotta go, or else we all lose."

Jasmine put out her blunt and placed it in an ashtray that was on top of a table near the window, and then she went and sat back down on the bed.

I sat down next to her. "So what's the deal?" I asked her.

"I can't kill anyone! I just know I can't, Nico. Can't you find someone else? Why do I have to do it? You got a whole army out there."

I began massaging her shoulders, which were stiff. "Jasmine, you don't gotta do anything you don't want to do. I asked because you're the only one I can trust. The fewer people who know, the better. I just told you those peoples are right around the corner and they don't knock on doors—they kick them in."

Jasmine began to tremble uncontrollably. "I just hate him so much that I can't understand why this decision isn't easier for me."

"He put his hands on you, didn't he?"

She shook her head, emphatically.

"Jasmine, don't ever lie to me again. I can look at you and see he hurt you. When we were making love I could feel your body tense up from pain when I'd grab your waist or arms. Tell me what he did to you."

Jasmine looked aloof. Instead of answering me, she said something better. "Just tell me how to pull it off, and I'm with it."

I looked at her, slowly nodding my head.

"Don't shit on me if I do this for you, Nico. Just promise me that."

"I put that on everything," I assured her. "I got you."

CHAPTER 15

Mia

By the time the sun rose and Nico still wasn't home, I knew he was going to stand me up and not make it to the spa date I had planned for us. Regardless of the comfortable lifestyle that being with Nico afforded me, I was getting so tired of the blatant disrespect, I had been seriously considering leaving him.

Many people thought I was just with Nico for his money. Was his money a good thing? Absolutely it was. But I was with him because I sincerely loved him. Now I was getting to the point where I was going to have to make a decision. Either leave and do me, or stay and tolerate his cheating ways and his lack of respect for me.

At seven in the morning I was still laying in bed, feeling a bit depressed. I flipped on the television. I was thinking about calling my girlfriend Sharmel and telling her that something had come up with Nico, and asking her if she would take his place and go with me to the salon. I was sure Sharmel was probably comfortable and cuddled up next to her man and probably didn't feel like going, but if I called her, I knew she would have agreed to go with me, since she understood how I often felt like a lonely widow.

Before I could make up my mind on what to do, I heard the doorbell ringing. Immediately I got nervous and started to think back to the break-in that had occurred. My cell phone started to ring, and I felt at ease when I recognized it was the armed security guard that Nico had hired. He was calling to tell me that it was safe to answer the door.

I smiled and quickly hopped out of the bed. I threw on my slippers and ran downstairs to open the door. Although I only had on a nightie, I didn't bother to throw on a robe because I was certain it was Nico at the door, making good on his promise and surprising me with roses or something. When I got to the door, I didn't even look through the glass partition to see who it was, and I just opened it with a smile and eager anticipation.

My smile quickly evaporated when I saw two white guys in suits standing at my front door.

"Can I help you?" I asked as I quickly positioned myself behind the door to hide my body. Only my face was exposed as I peered around the door.

One of the white men slid his suit jacket to the side and exposed his gold badge that was clipped to his belt buckle. He introduced himself and his partner and told me that they were detectives with the New York City Police Department and that they were looking to speak with Nicholas Carter.

"What is this about?" I asked.

"Miss, is Mr. Carter available?" the lead detective asked.

"No, he's not."

"Is he home?"

"I just said no," I replied with an attitude.

"Do you know when you can expect him home?"

"You asking a lot of questions, and I'm just trying to find out what this is in reference to." I chuckled, out of nervousness and disgust.

"His fingerprints were found on spent shell casings at a crime scene in Queens, and we just want to ask him some questions with regard to that," the detective explained to me in a matter-of-fact manner.

"What?" I said, a frown of confusion on my face.

"Miss, do you mind telling me your name?" the detective asked.

"Mia," I replied short and crisp.

"Can you give me your last name and your relation to Mr. Carter?"

"You know what? I'd rather not because I don't know what the hell is going on."

The detective nodded his head. He reached inside his pocket and handed me his card. "Can you give that to Mr. Carter and tell him to give me a call?"

I looked at the detective's card and nodded my head, answering his question.

"Thank you. Sorry to disturb you so early. You have a good day," the detective said to me, and him and his beefy muscular partner turned and walked off to their unmarked car and left.

After I locked the front door, I went up to the kitchen, grabbed the home cordless phone, and dialed Nico.

Nico didn't pick up. I kept calling him repeatedly for ten minutes straight, and he still didn't pick up.

"This is what I can't take!" I said out loud to myself.

I opened up the refrigerator, got a bagel, and put it in the toaster. While I waited for it to finish toasting, I picked up the home phone, and again I started to blow up Nico's phone. And still I got no answer.

I refused to leave a message that he wasn't going to even listen to.

After my bagel finished toasting, I put some butter on it and a little bit of jelly, and I put it on a small plate and took it upstairs to my bedroom, where I started to eat it. I grabbed my cell phone and called Nico, and he still wouldn't pick up. I took another bite of my bagel. I was about to slam my cell phone down, but I maintained my composure and sent him a text message.

I'm not calling you about our spa appointment if that's why you are ignoring my calls. Just trying to tell you a detective was just here at the house. CALL ME!

After I sent that message I finished eating my bagel and then I went back downstairs to my kitchen and put the dish in the sink and poured myself some orange juice. Just as I took a sip of the orange juice, I heard my doorbell ringing again.

When I went to open the door, I saw the security guard standing there.

"Nico wants to speak to you," he said and handed me a cell phone.

"What?" I shook my head as I took hold of the phone. "Hello?" I said.

"Mia, what's up?" Nico asked, sounding a bit nervous.

"What do you mean, what's up? Why do you never pick up your phone? I'm so tired of that, Nico!"

Nico was quiet for a moment, and then he asked, "A cop was at the crib?"

"Not *a* cop. *Two* cops were just here looking for you. And that's what you care about, right? Fuck me and fuck our spa date that we had. It's all about you."

"Mia, I'm sorry, a'ight?"

"No, it ain't *a'ight*! Sorry don't keep me safe and warm at night. And sorry don't make up for all your broken promises and lack of attention."

Nico shouted into the phone, "Mia, you know I'm out here scrambling. I'm handling business. I ain't out here bullshitting!"

I kept quiet because there was nothing else really for me to say.

"Now what did the cop say?"

I sighed and sucked my teeth. "He said that they had your prints on spent shell casings that were found at a crime scene in Queens and that they wanted to speak to you about it. I didn't answer none of their questions and when they saw that they were annoying me, they gave me their card to give to you and then they left."

"What the fuck?"

"I'm sorry," I said to the security guard, who was standing there the entire time, since it was his cell phone that me and Nico were talking on. I was sure that Nico didn't want to use his phone or call me on the house phone out of fear that those phones were tapped.

"You said they left you a card? What does it say?" Nico asked.

I walked over and retrieved the card from on top of the fireplace mantle where I had placed it.

"It says, 'Detective Peter Schwartz, NYPD Homicide Division 103rd Precinct,' and it has his contact numbers on it."

"Homicide?" Nico asked out loud. "What the fuck is that about?"

"Just call him and see," I said.

Nico didn't respond.

"So where are you anyway?"

"In the city."

"Where at in the city? So you wasn't even planning on coming home or even calling me? Unreal!"

"Mia, if there was ever a time when I don't need to hear your mouth, it's now! You see all the shit I got going on and that I'm dealing with and you beefin' over a fuckin' spa appointment? Calm the fuck down!"

I shook my head and sucked my teeth.

"Well, it ain't no sense in running up the minutes on this man's phone. I guess I'll see you when I see you."

"Go the fuck on with that bullshit, Mia! Hand the nigga his phone back then." Nico hung up without saying bye or anything.

"Thank you. Here you go," I said to the security guard as I handed him his phone. I started to tear up and cry.

"Is everything OK?" he asked.

"Yes," I said, nodding my head and wiping tears from my eyes. "I'll be OK. Everything is OK. Thank you," I said before closing and locking my front door.

I went back upstairs to my bedroom, got in my bed, turned off the TV, and pulled the covers over my head. There was five thousand dollars in cash sitting on my dresser. I knew I could spend that money on myself however I pleased. But as I cried myself to sleep, I really didn't care about that money. All I cared about was being happy, and I knew that money couldn't buy me happiness.

CHAPTER 16

Jasmine

When I opened my eyes from sleeping, I saw Nico standing on the other side of the room, staring out the window.

"Hey, good morning, babe," I said, yawning and stretching.

Nico turned around.

"I thought you would be long gone."

"Nah. I wouldn't just bounce on you like that. I had stepped out real quick to make a call from one of the pay phones downstairs."

"Pay phone?" I pulled the bed sheets up to my neck and turned on my side, which was still sore from the beatdown Shabazz gave me, to make myself comfortable.

"Yeah, Mia was blowing up my phone. She texted me about some detectives who came to the crib looking for me this morning. I ain't know what was up, so I called the security guard at my crib, and he gave the call to Mia. I just didn't want to be talking on my phone until I knew what was up."

"Oh, definitely." I sat up. "Did she say what was up?"

"It sound like some bullshit, but it ain't nothing."

I knew Nico was purposely not telling me any of the details, so I didn't press him on it. I got out of the bed and walked my naked body to the bathroom, so I could brush my teeth. While I brushed my teeth, Nico went back to looking out the window, apparently deep in thought about something. I was deep in thought as well. Did we really have a conversation last night about killing Shabazz? And most importantly, did I really agree to do it? One thing was for certain, which was Nico wasn't lying about the heat closing in.

After brushing my teeth, I walked out of the bathroom and crept up behind Nico. I put my arms around him and hugged him from behind. "You want a massage, baby?" I asked him.

"Nah, I'm good."

I grabbed him by the hand and walked him over to a chair, where I sat him down and began to massage his shoulders. "You gotta take time for yourself and just relax. I love giving massages," I said as I continued to rub his shoulders. As I massaged him, it was like I could feel the tension leaving his body. "It feels OK?"

"Yeah, it's on point."

"I can give you a full body massage if you want," I said.

"Not now. Maybe later. Yo, I'm still thinking about Mia stressing me more about why I didn't come home than she was about the detectives and what they wanted. She was blowing up my muthafuckin' phone. I was surprised that shit ain't wake you up."

"When I sleep, I'm usually out cold," I said, continuing to massage his shoulders. "I don't be hearin' nothing." Standing behind him, I slipped both of my hands inside his shirt and began to massage his chest. "This is what you would come home to every day if I was with you." I leaned over and I kissed him on his neck.

Nico nodded his head, but he didn't say anything.

"From a woman's perspective, I'm telling you, Mia is just with you for your money. She want you out here on these streets hustling and getting that money, but she ain't really a rider. She's selfish, I'm telling you. Women know women."

"You a rider though, right?"

I stopped massaging him. I walked around the chair, so that I was standing in front of him, and sat on his lap. I gave him a peck on his lips. "I'm gonna prove it to you that I am." As I started to kiss on Nico's neck, I could feel his dick getting stiff.

"So what you doing later?"

"Nothing really. I just gotta call Carlos and see what's up with this video shoot he supposedly booked me for."

"That's not what you doing."

I looked at him with a confused look as I continued to sit on his lap. "Whatchu mean?" My heart skipped a beat because I thought he was going to mention Shabazz and the murder plot.

"What you're gonna do is get dressed, and we both gonna go down to the heliport near Wall Street and we gonna charter a helicopter and have it fly us to Atlantic City so we can eat breakfast, and so I can take you to the outlets they got out there and let you go shopping."

"Oh my God! Are you serious?" I asked Nico, a huge smile on my face.

He smiled back at me and nodded his head yes, and then I gave him a hug that was firm and tight, like I didn't want to let go.

"I never been on a helicopter in my life! I'm so excited," I said as I stood up from Nico's lap.

"It's your birthday weekend, right?"

I smiled. "Yes."

"This is what I do for people who ride for me."

"You don't have to do this, Nico."

"I know that, but I wanna do it."

I didn't waste any more time. I grabbed my phone and hit Carlos up. I told him I was in Atlantic City and didn't know what time I was coming back, and that I would hit him up later. It being early, he probably wouldn't have seen my text until later, but I sent it anyway, just to get it out of the way.

Nico and I both took showers and got dressed. Then he called the heliport and paid for the helicopter via his credit card, and after I checked out of the hotel, we made our way downtown to the heliport in a cab.

I didn't know there was such a thing as a stylish helicopter, but the helicopter we found ourselves on was absolutely beautiful with plush leather seats. It didn't take long for us to be strapped in and to lift off. Throughout the entire time, I was cheesing and excited like a kid on Christmas morning as I looked out the window.

"The city skyline looks so beautiful," I said.

Nico nodded his head to me, but he seemed distracted by his phone as he read a text message and shook his head.

"Everything OK?" I asked.

"Yeah," he replied. "Excuse me, pilot, is it OK to use my cell phone?"

"Sure, that's not a problem, sir."

Nico immediately called Mia.

"Yeah, it's legit," Nico said in response to something Mia had asked him. "For me," he said after a pause. "Atlantic City," he said after another pause.

Nico was then quiet for a minute. I could see in his face that he was getting vexed.

"Mia, I'm not going through this back-and-forth shit with you! Get the fuck off my phone!" He then pressed End on his cell phone.

"What happened?"

"The credit card fraud department called the crib asking if the charge for the helicopter was legit, and Mia answered the call."

"I'm sorry, baby. I feel like I'm bringing you stress."

"What you apologizing for? It's just Mia and her bullshit."

I didn't have a response, so I kept quiet. Thankfully, before long we were in Atlantic City and preparing to land.

"We here already?"

"It's so much better than that two-hour-driving bullshit, right?"

"It doesn't even compare! You gonna spoil me, Nico." I smiled as I leaned over and gave him a kiss on the cheek. "Thank you again."

Nico nodded his head. Just then his phone began vibrating, and he said it was his man BJ. He answered the call, and it was clear that he was talking in code.

As Nico spoke on the phone, we had fully landed, and the pilot had opened the door and was escorting us out.

"Did you enjoy the flight?" the pilot asked me.

I smiled and replied, "Loved it!"

"Watch your step and watch your head," the pilot warned me.

While speaking to BJ, Nico reached in his pocket and pulled out a hundred-dollar bill and handed it to the pilot as a thank-you and a tip. The pilot said thank you to Nico and gave him a thumbs-up sign.

We walked to a Lincoln Town Car taxi and got in. Nico told the driver to take us to the outlets near the 40/40 club. Almost at the exact same time that the driver pulled off, I got a text message from Mia:

Have fun in Atlantic City and make sure you put all your chips on red.

I shook my head and was about to show the text to Nico, but I didn't. Mia didn't know for sure where I was at and was probably just testing my response. I was so tempted to just totally ignore her, but something in me wouldn't let the opportunity pass to take a stab at her.

OK I'll make sure I do that right after we finish shopping.

Mia immediately replied back to me:

Chyna, I may lose battles, but I always win the war!

Immediately my heart started pounding because I had no idea how she knew about my escorting name. *If she tells Nico anything about me prostituting myself, it's a wrap for me.* I started wondering if she had already told Nico, and he was just playing with my head and fucking with me so he could use me to get at Shabazz for him.

Nico had just ended his call with BJ, and I was still panicking on the inside from what Mia had texted me. I had to think quick on my feet. Nico was quiet, and he seemed like he also had some heavy shit on his mind.

I massaged Nico's thigh and his knee, snuggling next to him and kissing him. "Can I tell you a secret?" I whispered into his ear.

Nico looked at me and nodded his head.

"I love your dick," I whispered into his ear.

Nico smiled. "That's the secret?"

"Yup. And I have another one too. Can I tell it to you?"

Nico nodded his head again.

"I want you to fuck me raw, with no condom," I whispered into his ear. I was testing what his response would be, because if he knew

I was out there selling my pussy on the Internet there was no way he would even think about fucking me raw.

Nico smiled, but he looked at me like he was trying to figure me out. "That's what you like?"

"Mmm-hmmm. And you would love the way my pussy feels without a condom," I whispered to him as we pulled up to the outlets.

Nico went into his pockets and paid the driver. "So we'll make it happen," he said to me just before we exited the car.

"You promise?"

Nico looked at me. "It's on."

I smiled, feeling a little bit of relief. But I still had to respond to Mia, so I sent her a text.

My name is Jasmine bitch! And for the record the war is already won because I captured your king! Now kiss my muthafuckin ass!

My heart pounded because I had no idea how Mia was going to respond. Nevertheless, she never did respond to my text, and in many ways she was torturing me by not responding because I had no idea what she was up to or what her next move was.

Needless to say, I couldn't really enjoy the day shopping and gambling with Nico like I wanted to, simply because my mind was preoccupied with Mia knowing my secret.

I had no idea how she knew and who she planned on telling. Mia was quickly becoming a pain in my ass, so I knew I had to find a way to silence her ass quickly.

CHAPTER 17

Nico

I didn't want too much time to pass where Jasmine would get cold feet and change her mind about going through with the hit on Shabazz. When we came back from Atlantic City, I made sure I stayed in contact with her as much as I could, reassuring her that everything was going to be all right. I also made sure I gave her pocket money to keep her stable for a moment. She'd stressed the grand that Shabazz had supposedly taken, so I gave her two stacks. She grinned like a Cheshire cat.

The plan I had come up with was for Jasmine to get in touch with Shabazz and make him think that she really wanted to see him because she was now in fear for her life. That I had been coming around the crib, almost stalking her, and that I had changed, drastically. And then when they were in each other's presence, and the timing was right, she would lullaby his ass. Up close and personal.

Three days after we came back from Atlantic City, Jasmine called Shabazz from a prepaid cell phone I had purchased for her, and she was able to convince him to meet her at an IHOP restaurant on Rockaway Boulevard in Queens. I wasn't too happy about her meeting with him in a public place, but Shabazz wouldn't have it any other way. He was paranoid and rightfully so.

I told Jasmine to call me on my own prepaid cell phone and to put the phone on speaker mode and keep it in her Gucci bag, so I could hear everything that was being said while she was with him.

I was parked in the parking lot of a Burger King down the block from IHOP because I didn't want to be too far away, just in case something went wrong. It wasn't late, but it was dark outside. That 'dark' element had been my part of the plan. It would be best to meet when it was dark because I didn't want to take the chance that any parking lot or store cameras would be able to capture Jasmine's face on video if the cops were to ever try and review camera footage near the crime scene.

From the Burger King parking lot, I could see Jasmine's father's car. She had me on speaker phone, and even though her phone was in her bag, I could hear her clearly.

"You good?" I asked her.

"I'm high as a kite, and my heart is beating a mile a minute," Jasmine responded.

"Just remember how we said it should go down. Ten minutes from the time he shows up, it'll be done."

"OK, OK. I see his truck pulling into the lot now," Jasmine said to me. "I don't want him to get out the truck. Stay quiet, all right?"

I made sure I was quiet. I heard Jasmine's car door close, and I could hear and see her walking to Shabazz's truck.

"Hey, stranger," Jasmine said to Shabazz just as he stepped out of the truck.

It looked as if Shabazz gave Jasmine a kiss on the lips, and right after that she asked him if they could go back inside his truck for a minute.

"For what?" I heard Shabazz reply.

"Because I wanna talk to you about something, and I don't want everybody in our business."

"You did what I said and looked in your mirrors on your way over here, right?"

"Yeah, I wasn't followed. I'm sure of that. I made a left hand turn, then another left, and then another left just as you said. No other cars did that too."

I don't know if Shabazz said anything in response, but the next thing I heard was the sound of car doors opening and closing. I could tell that they were back inside the truck.

"What's up?" Shabazz asked Jasmine.

"What's up is, that shit you did to me in New Jersey was fuckin' foul!"

"Jasmine, it is what it is. Now, is this why you got me out here? Because, if it is, we can end this shit right now, and I can bounce. Fuck this IHOP shit, for real."

"Why you gotta be so cold about shit? You don't even care about the psychological scars I got because of you."

"Jasmine, I didn't come here to be put on no guilt trip. You said that the nigga Nico been harassing ya ass, now give me the 4-1-1 on that or I'ma bounce!"

Jasmine yelled, "You know what? Fuck it! Forget it then! You get on my fuckin' nerves!"

"Now do you see why I stopped calling your crazy ass?"

"No, this picture is why you stopped calling my ass!"

I was sure she had showed Shabazz the picture of him fucking some other bitch.

"Where the fuck you get that shit from?" Shabazz yelled. "You still fuckin' that nigga ain't you?"

"Who the fuck is this bitch? And how the hell was you playing me like that?"

"Jasmine, get the fuck out my truck!"

"I ain't going nowhere!" she yelled.

"Get the fuck out my shit, or I swear on everything, I will whip your ass!"

"You'll never put your hands on me again, Shabazz!"

At that point I could hear what sounded like tussling, and I heard Jasmine scream. Then I heard three consecutive gunshots.

"Oh my God! Oh shit! I can't believe this," Jasmine said.

After that everything went quiet, and the call ended. I wanted to call Jasmine back, but I didn't. I started up my car and pulled out of the Burger King parking lot, and as I drove past IHOP I could see her hurriedly getting into her car and quickly pulling off.

A few minutes later, my phone started to ring.

"Nico, what the hell did I just do?" Jasmine asked me.

"We good. Stop thinking. He was a dirty nigga. Don't worry about nothing. Just drive to Baisley Park and meet me there."

Baisley Park was only five minutes away. When I got there, Jasmine was already there and in tears.

"Give me the gun," I said.

After Jasmine handed it to me, I walked fifteen yards into the park and threw the gun into this large pond, and then I walked back over to her.

"We good! Stop crying," I said to Jasmine, hugging her.

"Nico, I just killed somebody."

"Don't nobody know shit, and we gonna keep it that way, a'ight?"

Jasmine looked up at me and nodded her head as she continued to cry.

I wiped her tears away. "I told you I got you, right? And I meant that shit."

"OK," Jasmine said in a soft voice.

"Go home, get a bunch of paper towels and alcohol, and wipe down the steering wheel of your father's car, and make sure you take a shower. You do that, and no gun residue can be traced back to you. The weapon is gone, so they don't got shit. They'll run Shabazz's background, and they'll know he was from the streets, and this whole shit will go away before it even starts."

Jasmine kept quiet for a moment and so did I and then she gave me a strong hug.

"Do you love me, Nico?"

I looked at her and gave her a kiss on the lips. "You know I do."

Jasmine then hugged me even tighter, and before long we both were going our separate ways. I had to give it up to Jasmine. She was definitely a rider!

CHAPTER 18

Mia

I didn't even respond to Jasmine's text message about the war already being won because she had captured the king. I knew exactly what she was trying to say, and I would be lying if I said I didn't feel chumped, cheap, played, used, and disrespected.

I also knew that getting back at Jasmine was going to be easy. I was going to start by printing up flyers of her Craigslist ads and then pay some Mexicans to put the flyers on all the cars near her house and near her school. To expose her whorish snake ass, I was also going to purchase a billboard near the busy Jamaica Avenue shopping district in Jamaica, Queens, which wasn't too far from where she lived.

I wanted Nico to find out about Jasmine's secret life on his own. I didn't want nothing coming directly from me because I felt that he would be more likely to kick her ass to the curb if he found out about her secrets from an outside party.

After Jasmine had sent that response text to me, I decided it was stupid for me to just lay in the bed sulking, crying, and depressed. I got out of the bed and called my home girl Sharmel and told her part of what had been going on, and that I just needed to get away for a few days. Sharmel knew that meant that I wanted her to get away with me. She readily accepted my offer of an all-expense-paid getaway to Miami for the both of us.

If it had been up to me, as soon as Sharmel said that she would go with me, I would have booked our tickets for us to leave right then and there that night, no matter how much the plane tickets cost. But Sharmel couldn't leave until the next day, so I ended up going on to Expedia.com, where I booked our plane tickets, hotel stay, and car rental all for the next day.

Even after I booked the trip, as much as I tried to ignore and block out what Jasmine had said to me in her last text, I just couldn't let it go. There was a part of me that felt like I just had to put something out there to let her know that her actions weren't fazing me, even though they were. So instead of texting Jasmine directly, I decided to just go on Twitter and send out a tweet because I had a good strong feeling that if she wasn't following me on Twitter, then she was checking my Twitter page on a regular basis. I knew I would be able to send her a subliminal message in a language and tone that she would easily understand and let her know that shit was all good in my life, regardless if she was fucking my man.

I went back on to my computer and logged on to Twitter.com and sent out a tweet that said:

Heading to the Shelborne Hotel in Miami, me and my girl about to do it up real big down there in South Beach! So don't hate, stunt bitches!

I felt good after sending that text because it made me feel like I did actually have some sort of power and control over my life, and at the same time I knew it would sting Jasmine and her hating ass.

By the time Sunday evening came, Nico still wasn't home, and to be honest, I was kind of glad. I was also hoping that by the time I was to leave in the morning that he wouldn't be back. I wanted him to come home to an empty house and not find me there, making it seem like I had just totally vanished off the face of the earth for five days.

By five o'clock Monday morning Nico still wasn't back home, and I was already up, showered, dressed, out the door and in the car service on my way to the airport to meet up with Sharmel.

Our flight wasn't scheduled to take off until eight o'clock that Monday morning, but we wanted to arrive at the airport extra early just because we knew the airport would be packed with people, it being a Monday. It turned out that even though the airport was crowded, we were able to check in right away, and we made it quickly through the different screening checkpoints.

Sharmel and I ate breakfast at a small eatery located inside the airport terminal, and then it seemed like before we could blink it was time for us to start boarding the plane. And almost on cue as we were about to board our flight, Nico began blowing up my phone. I purposely kept sending him to voice mail just so he could see how it felt to be on the other end of the disrespect.

"Nicholas Carter doesn't even exist to me for the next five days," I laughed and said to Sharmel right before turning off my phone and boarding the plane.

"You ain't say nothing but a word. You know how I do. I ain't calling to check in with my man either, so it's all good. I just hope you can keep up with me." Sharmel gave me a pound, and we both laughed as we made it to our second-row seats on the plane.

Our first-class seats definitely helped to make for a smooth flight. When we landed I picked up the Chevy Tahoe I had rented, and seeing that I had told Sharmel not to bring any luggage, the first thing we did even before checking into our hotel was go shopping.

I bought Sharmel and myself two different outfits for every day we were going to be in Miami, and I also bought us nice two-piece suits, one for the beach and a separate one for the hotel pool.

We shopped for about five hours, and it was tiring, but at the same time, it was fun and stress relieving. After we tore up the malls, we made it over to the resort hotel and checked in to our room, which had a balcony and an amazing view of the ocean.

"You did the damn thing by picking this spot!" Sharmel said to me, looking around the room. "You been to this hotel before?"

"I been to Miami before, of course, but never to this hotel. But I had kept hearing about how nice it is, and I was saying to myself that the next time I came down here that this is where I was going to stay."

As soon as I said that, my cell phone started to ring. It was Nico, and again I ignored him. "You see how guys are? The moment you start ignoring them, that's when they want to get all lovey-dovey and start caring and chasing behind you."

"Don't pick up for him."

"Pick up? I'm not even thinking about him. All I know is, we about to get dressed and go downstairs and have some drinks at the bar and then get nice and tanned."

And that was exactly what we did. We both threw on the brand-new bikinis I had just purchased and we made our way down to the pool area, where we reserved two deck chairs. After we had picked the perfect spot, we went over to the bar and ordered ourselves some drinks.

I said to Sharmel, "Make sure you watch out for me because you know how I get when I drink. And tonight, I plan on getting so twisted that it's not even funny."

"I got your back. Don't worry."

Our drinks arrived, and we started to sip on them. Sharmel told me that we needed to take trips like this more often.

"So true," I replied. "Especially in the winter time when it's thirty degrees and snowing in New York we could be somewhere nice and tropical like this instead of dealing with the drama."

"I still can't get over that chick selling her pussy on the internet," Sharmel said to me, changing the subject.

"Oh my God! You know how you just can't stand somebody? I can't stand her. I knew she was the jealous, hating type from the first day she saw me in my Range Rover. She was just giving off this negative energy. I should have known from then."

"Guys are gonna be guys. Everybody knows that. And there ain't shit we can do about it, especially when you got lowlife, gutter-ass chicks like Jasmine just looking to make a come-up at any cost." Sharmel said just before sipping on her margarita.

"Hello, ladies," a tall, dark-skinned muscular dude said to me and Sharmel, interrupting our conversation but not in a rude way.

"Hello," we both replied, I couldn't help but smile as I looked in his direction with my designer shades on.

"I don't know what the two of you are doing tonight, but I'm one of the owners at Mansion nightclub, and I would love for the both of you to come party with us. I'll make sure that y'all don't have to wait on the line or any of that. Drinks and everything is on me, since I assume that both of you are from New York." He smiled.

I smiled back. "How do you know we're from New York?"

"It's the swagger and the sophistication. Y'all both got it. I seen y'all when you walked onto the deck and I was like, 'They gotta be from New York.'"

"Actually, we are from New York. I'm Sharmel, and this is Mia."

"I'm Kelvin." Kelvin extended his hand to the both of us, his baby-oiled muscles glistening in the sunlight. He was wearing swimming trunks, flip-flops, and a pair of shades.

"I don't have any cards on me, as you can see. I don't even have my phone with me, but I can give you my number. And if y'all free, hit me up and come through, and I'll make sure y'all both have a good time. DJ Stevie J will be doing the music. He always shuts it down up in there. And like I said, I'll comp y'all on everything."

"How could we turn that down? I heard a lot of good things about Mansion." I shook Kelvin's hand.

Kelvin made a bit more small talk before he went to one of the deck chairs and sat down to read a magazine.

Laughing, I said to Sharmel, "Now he could *definitely* get it!"

"Don't get that wild down here."

I laughed it off and told her that I wouldn't, and I also reminded her that it was just the liquor talking for me.

Later on that evening, I ended up calling Kelvin to remind him we would definitely be there. He told me he would make sure we was on the list, and all we had to do was go to the front of the line and let them know our names, and if we had any problems, we just had to call him and he would take care of it.

"Something urgent came up, so I might be getting there late. But regardless I'll try to find you. If I do, I'll buy you and your girl a bottle of whatever y'all wanna drink," Kelvin said before ending the call.

When me and Sharmel made it inside the club, I instantly saw what all the hype concerning Mansion was about. The huge club was packed, but it didn't feel ghetto, where everybody is all rammed up together like sardines. And I also liked that the club wasn't just full of black people, it also had white people, Asians, and Latinos. The vibe inside the club was just what I was looking for as an escape from New York.

Sharmel wasn't shy by nature, and after enough drinks my shyness had disappeared, so it didn't take long for the two of us to warm up to the music and start dancing. Before long Sharmel had a guy come up to her, and without asking for permission he started to dance with her. He was a cute guy, but he was shorter than Sharmel. I knew how much Sharmel hated short dudes so it was funny to watch him interact with her.

I stepped off so as not to crowd them, and when the guy's back was to me, I laughed at Sharmel, gesturing with my hand to indicate how short the guy was.

As I continued to dance by myself, I looked over to my right and could have sworn I saw a chick who looked just like Jasmine. But then I figured I had to just be bugging out, that there was no way Jasmine was down there. At that point, I needed a drink. I walked up to Sharmel and told her I was going over to the bar, pointing to the area.

As soon as I made it to the bar, Sharmel came up to me.

"Thank God! You gave me an excuse to get away from Mighty Mouse," she said, and we both started laughing.

"I had to get a drink. I swear I just saw a chick who looked just like Jasmine, and I was saying, 'I gotta get that heifer off my mind,'" I explained to Sharmel just before ordering us two Cosmopolitans.

While we sat at the bar drinking, I saw Kelvin walk by with two other dudes.

"There goes the dude from the hotel from this morning," I said to Sharmel.

Sharmel wanted me to run up on Kelvin and his friends. But just because he had put us on the VIP list, I didn't want to come across like a needy stalker or something, so I told her we needed to just chill and have a good time and not be intrusive.

"It's still early. Later on tonight I'll text him and see where he's at," I said to Sharmel.

We continued to drink and party and have a really good time. As time went on, the club got more and more packed. LeBron James and his entourage had showed up in the club. The chick from the TV show, *The Game*, showed up, and there were other celebrities that kept getting shout-outs from the DJ, but I couldn't keep track of all the names.

We had been in the club for a good three hours, by which time I was really feeling nice from all the liquor I had drunk. Sharmel didn't drink as much as I did, but she was enjoying herself, and getting way more male attention than I was. She had to have gotten close to three phone numbers from different dudes, and I was starting to feel self-conscious.

Just at the moment when I was thinking that maybe I was starting to lose some of my magic, Kelvin sent me a text message:

Hey beautiful, you still here? I didn't forget about those bottles. Hit me back.

I instantly texted him back and told him that we were still there and that I was on the first floor at one of the bars. Kelvin texted me right back and told me which area he was in.

I finished my drink and told Sharmel that Kelvin had just hit me up, and the two of us made our way through the club and up a huge sweeping staircase and over to where he was at.

When we got to the VIP area, Kelvin walked up to me with a cocktail waitress who had two bottles of champagne with large sparklers on them. It was definitely a good look.

"Did I keep my promise or what?" Kelvin said to me and Sharmel.

The sparklers definitely attracted attention, and people in the VIP area were looking at me and Sharmel, trying to figure out if we were celebs.

"Yes, you certainly did," I said to Kelvin.

The waitress popped the bottles for us and poured us some champagne, and as we drank, we made small talk with Kelvin.

"Normally we're closed on Monday and Tuesday, but it's Serena's launch party for her new handbags. That's why it's so packed up in here," Kelvin explained.

"Oh, we didn't even know. Serena Williams, the tennis player, right?" Sharmel asked.

"Yeah, that Serena," Kelvin said. "I'll try to get y'all a bag if they got any left. I didn't even think about it."

I was quiet for the moment and I continued to drink my champagne. It was wild because all of a sudden it seemed like I was like really drunk or something. The sound system seemed much more powerful than before. I could feel the bass of the music in my chest. Even the huge chandeliers that hung from the ceiling appeared larger than I had noticed before. It was just a crazy feeling.

Kelvin introduced us to two of his home boys and while they made small talk with Sharmel, he took me aside and he started to make private conversation with me.

"So you having a good time?" he asked.

I smiled and told him I was. Then I joked and asked him what he had slipped into my drink.

He smiled. "Why you say that?"

"I just feel super nice. I wasn't feeling like this when I was downstairs."

"It's just the lights and the music up here on this level is a little different, that's all."

"So you own this spot?"

"Yeah, me and my two partners. Years ago we started out as club promoters for a bunch of different clubs, and so this was just a natural move for us."

"That's real good." I drank some more champagne.

"So what about you? What do you do?"

I hated when people asked me that question because I never really had an answer that made sense to them.

"I'm a professional gold digger," I said with a smile.

Kelvin started to laugh. "You got a sense of humor. I like women who know how to laugh."

Then I decided to just keep it real with him. "You ever been to New York?" I asked.

"That's where I'm from. Co-op City in the Bronx!"

"Really? So you went from New York to owning a club down here in Miami?"

"Yup, and I live in Atlanta. So that's wild, right?"

"Very wild, but it's cool though. Well, since you from New York, you ever heard of Ghetto Mafia?"

"Of course."

"So then you probably heard of a dude named Nico?"

"I don't know him, but I heard the name, it rings out."

"Nico is my man, and he basically takes care of me."

The way I figured, there was no reason for me to lie. Kelvin was cute, and he was definitely my type, but I was never into playing games.

"So you're wifey," Kelvin replied. "I can see why."

"Why what?"

"Why a nigga would want to wife you. I mean, I definitely would."

That put a smile on my face.

"So what are y'all doing when y'all bounce?"

"I don't know. Why? What's up?" I asked, hoping not to come across needy.

Kelvin extended his hand to me, guided me toward him, and started to dance with me. He had no idea he was giving me the exact type of attention I had been craving, and he seemed like he was the perfect catch. I couldn't believe how good my cards were lining up.

"Don't take offense," Kelvin said to me. "But I asked because I want you to come back to the hotel with me."

He was about seven inches taller than me, so I had to look up at him. I smiled and I shook my head. "You are too much," I said into his ear.

"I'm just honest, that's all."

My cell phone started to vibrate right at that moment. I looked at it and noticed it was Nico.

Don't let me have to beat your ass!

I sucked my teeth and sighed when I saw that message. I just ignored it and continued to ignore Nico as I had been doing all along.

"I would go back to the hotel and chill with you, but you probably meet all kinds of women coming through here. And, as sexy as you are, I'm sure you sex everything that moves," I said.

Kelvin shook his head no.

"That's not true?"

"No, it's not. I'm a good dude."

I looked at Kelvin as I continued to two-step with him to the music.

"You want me to tell you something I see about you?" Kelvin asked me.

"Yeah, tell me."

"You're a loyal person, but what's going on is that you're hurting on the inside because you've been hurt."

I paused from dancing and looked at him in amazement. "How do you know that?"

"It's a gift."

"A gift? So you a psychic?"

"Nah, I'm not a psychic," Kelvin reached in and gave me a peck on my neck, his soft full lips sending shivers down my spine.

"You have to leave me alone." I gently pushed Kelvin away from me. I was feeling nice at that moment, and Kelvin was making me feel really good, but as mad and as disappointed as I was with Nico, I could never step out on him.

"A'ight, I'll leave you alone. But I want you to remember something."

"What's that?"

"Never say never."

"OK, now you're scaring me, and I can't even tell you why." I laughed and put both of my hands in the air in surrender. "Get away from me."

Kelvin smiled and asked me when I was leaving to go back to New York. I told him, and then he asked me if he could call me again.

"Yes, you can call me," I said to him before he walked off with his friends.

As soon as Sharmel came over to me, I said to her, "Remember when I said at the pool that he could get it?"

She laughed and nodded her head.

"Well, I don't even know his last name, but he is about to get it!"

"Mia, that's just that liquor talking for you," Sharmel replied as we made our way to another part of the club.

Maybe it was the liquor talking, but a half an hour later as I stood against one of the exposed brick walls inside Mansion nightclub, I decided to send Kelvin a text message.

What's your room number?

Kelvin texted me back five minutes later with his response: *726*

Maybe it was the liquor that was allowing me to enjoy flirting with Kelvin. Whatever it was, I sent a text back that said, *So what time can I meet you there?*

Kelvin quickly replied, *Meet me there at five a.m.*

At that time, it was close to three thirty in the morning and I didn't want to change my mind. I told Sharmel I wanted to get two more drinks and then we could leave. Sharmel was with my plan for more drinks, but she had no idea about my other plan to hook up with Kelvin.

The club was still rocking and didn't look like it was winding down anytime soon. Me and Sharmel had a tough time getting the attention of the bartender. But we finally did, and I ordered two more drinks for the both of us, to keep me buzzing and feeling nice until five a.m.

I sent back to Kelvin, *Ok, I'll be there.*

And, sure enough, at five a.m., against Sharmel's advice and warning, I found myself standing in front of Room 726, gently knocking on the door and waiting for Kelvin to open it up and let me in.

CHAPTER 19

Jasmine

Everything was working out just as I had planned and hoped. The only thing I forgot to do was to make sure that my iPhone was fully charged.

"This phone better not die on me," I said to Kelvin while we waited for Mia to show up at his room.

"You got like a quarter of the battery life left," Kelvin said to me. "You should be good. That shit should last you an hour at least."

Mia wasn't supposed to come to the room until five, but she was knocking at Kelvin's door at a quarter to five.

"That's her!" I whispered to Kelvin. I scrambled to hide my shoes and my bag, so Mia would have no reason to get suspicious. After I hid my stuff, I scurried over to the closet and positioned myself inside, and Kelvin partially closed the two-door closet behind me.

Mia knocked on the hotel room door again, and this time Kelvin opened it. I started the video recorder on my iPhone, and although I couldn't actually start filming anything just yet, I still wanted the recorder going, just in case Mia said something I wanted to have on tape.

"You got here quick," Kelvin said.

"Yeah, after I sent you that text, I just had two more drinks with my girl, and then we left," Mia replied.

Kelvin escorted her into the room. "Oh, OK. So you want another drink? I brought some champagne back from the club, and I got some orange juice, if you wanna mix it."

Mia said that she wanted some but had to use the bathroom first. She went to the bathroom and stayed in there for about three minutes, and she came out and started to drink the mimosa Kelvin had mixed for her.

They made small talk about who they knew in New York and how old they were and what high school they went to and all of that. All the while they continued to drink, I could tell that the drinks were definitely affecting Mia, because she was getting more and more talkative.

She said to Kelvin, "I was just down here like the other week. I had to do a photo shoot for J-Lo."

"That's where the fuck I know you from! You a model, right?"

Mia told him that she was, and that she was also trying to get into acting.

"So why didn't you say that in the club? You was making it seem like you just live off of your man's money."

"Please don't mention my man to me. I'm so not feeling him right now."

I was so glad I had that on tape.

At that point I guess Kelvin used that as his cue to make his move because I heard what sounded like kissing. I slowly opened the door a little bit more and took a chance and peered out, and sure enough Mia and Kelvin were kissing. I made sure that I was capturing it all.

"You so fuckin' sexy," Mia said to Kelvin as he took off his shirt. Then Mia pushed him away, and she stood up and walked to the other side of the room.

I had to be real careful that she didn't turn around and see me. Not wanting to take any chances, I went back inside the closet.

"Why you pushing me away?"

"Because I don't even know your last name."

"It don't matter because I don't know yours either, and nobody knows that we're here but me and you."

I peeked out the closet again in time to see Kelvin pushing up on Mia. He gave her a peck on the lips, and she felt on his six-pack while drinking champagne straight from the bottle.

"Take your heels off," he said to Mia, which she did.

"I got pretty feet, don't I?" Mia drank some more of her mimosa.

After Mia took off her shoes, Kelvin walked up to her and unbuttoned her shorts. Then he slipped his hands inside and started playing with her pussy.

Mia closed her eyes while being touched by Kelvin. "I don't know you after tonight," she said to him.

Kelvin put up one finger to his mouth and told Mia to shush because she was talking too much. Then he slid her out of her shorts and then her thong.

"You gotta ask me, if you can fuck me," Mia playfully said to Kelvin. She gently smacked him on the face.

"Can I fuck you?"

"Say it like you really want it!"

I almost started laughing. I didn't know she was into role playing.

"Can I fuck you, baby?" Kelvin said a little more forcefully.

Mia then reached for her shorts. "You don't really want this pussy."

"Can I fuck the shit outta your pussy, baby?"

"That's what I'm talking about." Mia started rubbing on Kelvin's dick.

Kelvin took his pants off, and his dick was standing firm and ready for action. He reached down into his pants pocket and got a condom and slipped it onto his dick.

Mia took the champagne bottle and took a swig from it. She gave Kelvin a real seductive look. I could tell she was drunk, but at the same time, she definitely seemed like she knew exactly what she wanted.

At that point my battery was really getting low. I was ready to scream. I was praying the phone didn't completely shut off on me. And I was also praying that Kelvin would hurry up and put his dick inside Mia, so I could have what I needed to hang her ass.

Mia walked toward a chair and straddled it in a way where her knees were facing the back of the chair. It was clear that she wanted Kelvin to fuck her from the back, and the position she chose was perfect for me to film.

From the moment Kelvin slipped his dick inside Mia's pussy, she started talking shit. She just wouldn't shut the fuck up. Never in a million years would I have thought that little pretty and perfect Mia with the soft voice would have had such an X-rated potty mouth. It had to be the champagne and the liquor talking for her because it just seemed so way out of character for her.

Mia turned and said to Kelvin, "I wanna feel your balls slamming into my pussy!" Then she added, "Fuck me harder, you black muthafucka!"

Mia wasn't a screamer and a moaner, but she was definitely a shit-talker. It was so funny to me, I almost burst out laughing.

Kelvin wasn't saying nothing. He was just handling his business, fucking her.

"Pull my hair and fuck me deeper! You like this wet pussy?" Before Kelvin could even answer, she commanded him, "Smack my ass!"

I was almost in stitches. It was so hard for me to not laugh. I was seriously thinking about slipping out of the room completely just so I could go somewhere and laugh my ass off.

"I wanna feel every inch of that dick!" she barked, and began to moan loudly. "Deeper, baby! Deeper!"

I could tell Mia was about to come. When she came, her whole body stiffened, and she sounded like she was having an asthma attack, gasping for air. Her coming was literally the only thing that silenced her.

After Mia came, and Kelvin pulled his dick out, she sat down in the chair to catch her breath. She was having these little mini-tremors.

I was hoping Kelvin would take the condom off and make her suck his dick, but then I figured that he didn't because Mia would have been facing me.

"You can't quit on me now," Kelvin said.

Mia shook her head. She stood up and turned around, and Kelvin fucked her from the back standing up. He fucked her for about another two minutes, and then he pulled his dick out and pulled off the condom and shot his come all over Mia's back and ass.

Finally after all that talking Mia seemed like she was returning to normal.

Kelvin grabbed Mia by the hand and led her into the bathroom, giving me my moment to escape. I quickly and silently slid out of the room and trotted down the hallway and into a stairwell, where I let out the biggest, loudest, and longest laugh I ever had in my life.

At that point I knew none of it would have even come about if it hadn't been for Mia running her mouth on Twitter and telling the world where she was going to be staying.

When I saw her tweet, Kelvin was the first person I thought of to help me pull off my plan. I had known Kelvin from way back in the days. Me and him had never actually fucked because we knew each other for so long that we had developed a brother/sister kind of relationship. But I knew he would do anything for me, and on the flip side, I would do anything for him that he needed me to do.

Kelvin wasn't a part owner of Mansion, but he was so cool with the owners of the club, he had carte blanche to whatever he wanted at that club, when he wanted it. What he really did for a living was hustle coke and pills inside the club, so he had a ton of money and the right swagger that I knew Mia would fall for.

My whole plan was to fly down to Miami, which was what I did, and Kelvin agreed to pay for my room at the hotel, which was the same room he fucked Mia in. I knew Mia would be weak and vulnerable and would fall for Kelvin if he came at her the right way.

At that point I wasn't worried at all about what moves Mia would make, in terms of exposing my prostitution secret. I had what I needed to totally destroy her world, and that was exactly what I was going to do. The only thing I had to figure out was whether to strike first or to wait for her to make her move first and then go after her. Either way, I knew that as soon as Nico saw that tape, her ass would be official black history. Mia had no idea how I got down, but she was going to soon find the fuck out.

CHAPTER 20

Nico

I t was Saturday, almost a week after I had come back from Atlantic City with Jasmine, and Mia still wasn't home. I had to find out from Sharmel's man where Mia and her partner in crime had run off to. To be honest, I cared about the disrespect that Mia was showing me, but I had more important shit to deal with.

It was a few days since Jasmine had carried out the hit on Shabazz for me, and that morning my cell phone was ringing off crazy. Shabazz's murder had hit the morning news after he was found dead in his truck in the IHOP parking lot. When everybody called me, I played it off like I was shocked, like I had no idea who could have been behind it.

But by two o'clock that afternoon, Bebo called a meeting at the underground. I was shocked that even BJ had arrived before I did. It was clear that my name had been ringing out as a possible suspect in Shabazz's murder.

"What's good?" I said to everybody. I started to give everybody a pound.

Bebo didn't give me a pound, but he did give me a fist bump.

"That shit is fucked up what the news is showing about Shabazz," I said. I could feel that there was some kind of tension in the room, but I didn't exactly know why.

"Nico, you know I'm always straight up with you, and I always keep it one hundred," Bebo said with a slight screw face as he sat on the end of an old black leather couch.

"Bebo, what the fuck is up?" I asked.

Bebo stood up and walked to the other side of the room. He took out a Fanta leaf and started to roll some weed as he spoke, and wouldn't look at me directly.

"When you run around and make moves without niggas knowing what the fuck you doin', that's how shit gets fucked up," Bebo said.

"The fuck you talkin' 'bout?" I asked with obvious bass in my voice.

"I'm talking about you and BJ running around, making us look weak and desperate for product and shit, when we all agreed that we were gonna start eatin' off the same package with some other crews. How you fuckin' with them Haitians? Who sanctioned that, huh? Because I sure didn't."

"So then where the fuck is the product? My niggas was out here starving, and they lookin' to me to supply them with shit. Our connect dried up, so I'm doing what I gotta do so we can all keep eating," I responded.

"Nigga, we got the product. I know what the fuck I'm doing! We got the shit off the boat yesterday. You runnin' around chasing that weak shit, and I'm telling you, we got the best shit right now, and that's what the fuck this game has always been about. You want a hundred percent of a little bit of that weak-ass product 'cause yo' ass on that non-loyal shit!" Bebo said.

I shook my head. I held my tongue because I was about to spazz out on Bebo.

"You shakin' your head, but I got Homicide asking me why was your prints on the shell casings from the bullets that killed my nephew," Bebo said to me.

"What the fuck you talkin' 'bout? Yo, that's some bullshit, and them muthafuckas is lying! You and I both know if they really had my prints that my ass would be locked the fuck up, right now sitting on Rikers Island. So if you even thinking I had something to do with that shit, you straight bugging the fuck out."

The whole room was quiet.

Bebo looked at me like he was trying to burn a hole into my soul to see what I was thinking. He had finished rolling his blunt and started to take some pulls from it. He blew weed smoke out of his lungs. "You was fuckin' Shabazz's girl or what?"

"You a fuckin' federal agent or something, my nigga? You interrogating me?"

"Nah, I ain't no fed, but I'm just saying."

"You saying what?" I looked right at him and waited for his response.

Bebo was quiet, so I kept talking.

"If we got some bricks, then let's talk about chopping that shit up, and if not, then what the hell we really here for?" I said. "Shabazz was in the street just like all of us, so he knew what came with that. He got caught out there, and we'll deal with that. He was family. I'll make sure that his family is good. I already been on that from this morning," I said.

Bebo walked over to me and gave me a pound and a ghetto embrace. "We good. I just wanted to speak to you straight up. You know how I do," Bebo said.

"And you know I respect that. Now let's talk about who is knocking off our crew one-by-one," I said.

At that point in the meeting, everybody else in the room all got involved in the conversation, and I played everything cool but inside I was heated. What the fuck was taking BJ so long to dead that snitch muthafucka? Now that Shabazz got hit I was sure the alphabet boys were putting pressure on Bebo to set up the drug transaction with all the major players.

When I left that meeting I asked BJ what the hold up was.

"I'm on it, Nico, that's my word," BJ said reassuringly. "But I gotta do this shit right. You said make him disappear. Each time that nigga leaves his house he's either with Earl, or Corey, or both them niggas. I gotta catch him slippin', alone. If I fuck this up my life is at stake in more than one way. You feel me?"

I nodded. I knew BJ was right. We had to be smart about putting Bebo six feet under, or all of us would be spending the rest of our lives in a 6 x 6 jail cell.

CHAPTER 21

Mia

Friday afternoon me and Sharmel had returned home from our Miami getaway. Sharmel went home to her house, and I went home to mine. When I was down in Miami, I had felt totally free and liberated, but now that I was back in New York, the realities of things were starting to set in.

I had the biggest regrets for what I'd done with Kelvin, and I felt like the biggest slut in the world. But there was nothing I could do to change the past. I didn't feel too bad because although I had fucked Kelvin, I was at least smart enough to make sure I deleted his number from my phone. And I also made sure that he had deleted my number from his phone. This way there would be no way we could stay in contact with each other.

I would be lying if I said I didn't want to get to know Kelvin better. But the best thing was to keep that little tryst of mine buried in the past. Sharmel was my girl for life, so I didn't have to ever worry about her running her mouth to anyone about what I had done.

When I came home, Nico wasn't there, which gave me some time to clean the house, do laundry, and cook, so that when he did come home he would at least come home to a pleasant environment. And I cooked his favorite meal of collard greens, cornbread, black-eyed peas, and barbecue ribs.

My timing was perfect because almost as soon as I took the ribs out of the oven, Nico walked in the house. I had no idea what his reaction or response to me would be and I was prepared for anything.

Nico walked into the kitchen and didn't come up to me and give me a hug and a kiss like he usually did when he saw me.

"So you think you can just run off to Miami, not say shit to nobody and then come home and cook, and that's supposed to just smooth everything over?"

"Baby, I'm sorry but—"

"But nothing!" Nico said, cutting me off. "I don't wanna hear your shit right now!"

I shook my head, trying to stay calm, but all those feelings that I had before I went to Miami all instantly came back, but I held them in check.

"I cooked you some ribs and cornbread, if you wanna eat."

Nico walked out of the kitchen and went upstairs to our bedroom. I didn't know what to say, but I didn't want to have tons of tension in the house. So I waited a few minutes, and then I went upstairs to talk to him.

Nico was in the bathroom, and the water was running in the shower.

"You going out?" I asked.

"Yeah."

"You don't want anything to eat?"

"Nah, I'm good."

"Baby, listen. I was only ignoring your calls and texts because I wanted you to see how I feel when you shut me out," I said, trying my best to be humble. "But I'm sorry. Don't read any more into it, because it's nothing. OK?"

"We good."

"Are you sure, Nico?"

Nico looked at me and nodded his head.

"OK, so you sure you don't want something to eat?"

Nico ignored me.

"Do you want to hear about my trip?"

"Not really."

"See, you do have an attitude! Urrgggh!" I said. "Nico, just talk to me."

"There's nothing to fuckin' talk about!"

I blew some air out my lungs as I shook my head. "So can you tell me where you're going?"

"I'm going out."

"See, this is what I can't stand!" I yelled, storming out of the bathroom.

"Ain't nobody handcuffing you! You don't have to stand shit. You can fuckin' leave," Nico barked out to me.

Ignoring his threat, I went downstairs and fixed myself a plate of food, but my nerves were shot, and my body wouldn't let me eat anything. All I could do was sit there and pick at my food. I did that for close to a half an hour, until I heard Nico leave the house without even saying good-bye to me.

I went back upstairs to my room and found myself in a similar position that I had been in right before I'd left for Miami—in my bed with the covers over my head and tears streaming down my eyes.

The only difference was, at least now I had the fantasy thoughts of Kelvin running through my mind to help ease the pain I was feeling.

Even though I had deleted Kelvin's number from my phone, as I lay there crying in the bed, I thought about going online and logging on to my cell phone account and retrieving his number from my account log. I was sure, if I hit him up, he would be willing to fly up to New York and spend some time with me.

It took everything in me not to reach out to Kelvin, but ultimately I decided against it since I knew Nico was only acting the way he was because of Jasmine. It was definitely time for me to expose her whorish ways to Nico.

My only fear was that he would end up choosing her over me after I exposed her. But I had to do what I had to do because this sitting home-alone, sulking, and crying my eyes out was for the birds.

CHAPTER 22

Jasmine

The day before my trip to Miami, I lied and told Nico I was in Detroit attending my uncle's funeral. Too much had gone on over a few days, including going through with his plot to murder Shabazz.

Nico understood and, since I told him I would be back that Monday, he told me to just hit him up when I got back. He also told me that he was sorry to hear about my uncle's passing.

Well, when I got back from Miami, Nico didn't let any grass grow under my feet. He picked me up at around two in the afternoon and didn't let me out of his sight until he had dropped me off at my house that evening.

Honestly speaking, pulling that trigger and killing Shabazz was without a doubt one of the hardest things that I ever did in my life. I never thought I'd have the balls to actually pull the trigger. It seemed fake, at first. Like I could pull the trigger and then undo what was done as if it were a dress rehearsal. Only it wasn't. It was very real. I took a man's life. And two hours after the shooting, my nerves were still very much on edge, just like Nico had warned me they would be. I was trying my hardest to relax, but I just couldn't get out of my mind the image of Shabazz's shocked and fear-stricken face when I shot him. I needed to smoke some weed to calm my nerves, but I was going to wait until later that night when my parents went to sleep, and then I was going to go outside and smoke.

I was surprised and extremely annoyed when my father told me that Simone was at the door because the last thing I wanted at that moment was company. And I was surprised because Simone hadn't called me before coming over. Usually she would call me before stopping by. I had had a long birthday weekend, murdered Shabazz, and flew to Miami to secretly film Mia, so the last thing I felt like doing was entertaining. Reluctantly I told my father to let her in and to tell her to come upstairs to my room.

"Hey, girl," I said as I got out of the bed and put on my robe and turned on the TV. I had just come out of the shower, and since it was still early, I wasn't ready to go to sleep for the night. But I was drained and wanted to get a quick hour or two of sleep.

"Jasmine, what's going on?" Simone asked.

My eyes flew open in shock. "Why? What you heard?"

"Heard about what?" she asked, confused. "You've just been real distant with me lately and you're hardly ever around. I just want to know what's up. You got a new best friend or something?"

"Oh, that," I said, dismissively. "You know you're still my girl. I just got a lot going on."

"Like what?" She made herself comfortable on my bed.

"Like too much to discuss now." I gently grabbed her by her arm and guided her off my bed. "I'm really tired. I promise I'll hit you up tomorrow and we can hang out."

Simone looked hurt. But she'd get over it.

When she left, as I lay in the bed, I sent Nico a text message asking how he was doing. Thirty minutes went by, and he didn't respond to me. I just took that to mean he was busy, and I went to sleep.

I didn't hear from Nico for the rest of the night, but he called me late the next day.

"Hello."

"Jazzy, what's up?"

"Nothing. I'm just laying in the bed thinking," I said.

"About what?"

"You know . . ."

Nico was quiet, waiting for me to say something.

"But I'm a'ight."

"You not falling apart are you?"

"No, not at all."

"For your sake you bet' not be." Nico's statement hung in the air as a veil threat. It sent a chill down my spine.

"Of course I'm not," I stated. "Don't think like that."

"A'ight, I ain't stressin' that shit. But, yo, keep your phone on. I'll hit you back. I gotta bounce," Nico said.

When the call with Nico ended, my anxiety level was up. I was wondering what he was thinking. I didn't want him to think that I would one day open my mouth and snitch about Shabazz's murder.

I needed some weed in the worst way to calm my nerves, but I was down to my last few dollars and didn't want to be totally broke. I'd already blown the two g's Nico had given me on a pair of Christian Louboutins and a Fendi bag. I got up and paced around the house, and then I turned on the TV and started watching *The View*. It was still early, but it didn't matter. I went downstairs to my father's bar and poured myself some vodka and orange juice and took it back upstairs with me to my bedroom and drank it while I finished watching *The View*.

The vodka wasn't doing it for me, so after *The View* went off, I called in a weed order, and when my weed supplier came by my crib, I gave him the last fifty dollars I had. But it was the best way for me to calm down from all the thoughts running through my mind.

While I was getting high, I decided to post another online ad so that I could get some more money in my pocket. Only thing was, I had just spent my cab money and my four-hours' worth of motel money on the weed, so it didn't make sense to place the sex ad and not have money for the motel or even for the cab ride to get me there.

I sat butt naked on my bed and thought about what I should do. No ideas were coming to me, and I was reluctant to hit up Nico for any more dough. And although I knew Nico was good for some money, I didn't want him thinking that I was extorting him now that I had murdered Shabazz. That type of shit could get me killed.

While I continued to smoke, something hit me and told me to check the prepaid cell phone I used as my contact number specifically for turning tricks.

I had four messages when I checked the voice mail. Two were from guys I didn't even remember being with, and one was from a new prospective client who had seen one of my old ads online and was calling to see if I was available. But those three messages were more than a week old. The last message was from the white guy, Mike, who had left a message the night before.

"Hey Chyna, I don't know if you remember me, but this is Mike. No disrespect hun, so please don't take this as me being vulgar or anything. But I really want some more of that black nigger pussy of yours. I don't know if you're working or not tonight, but if you are, call me on my cell phone at 718-786-XXXX."

I called Mike back, and he picked up on the second ring.

"Mike?" I asked, just making sure it was him.

"Yes, this is Mike."

"Hey, Mike," I said, a smile on my face. "You still in the mood for some of this black nigger pussy?"

"Chyna?"

"Yeah, it's me."

Mike told me that he was just thinking about me and that he definitely wanted to see me. I hated feeling so desperate and putting myself in tough situations, but I had to do what I had to do. I told Mike that we couldn't meet at our regular spot and that my pimp had access to a house in South Jamaica that I was going to be working out of for the day but only up until three that afternoon, and that if he wanted to get some he would have to come through ASAP.

Within a half-hour Mike had showed up at the front door of my parents' house. I had removed all the pictures of myself and my family so that he wouldn't have any idea that I lived there, and I took him into the basement, where I had let out the couch bed.

I told Mike that it was going to be two-fifty for the hour instead of the price that he had paid before but that price was inclusive of the tip.

Mike paid me the money, and we got busy.

I had hit a new stress relieving low, but it was all good because I set my mind to something, and I had achieved my goal. But I knew if I wanted to leave the prostitution world alone forever, I would have to set my mind to an ever bigger goal, that being to lock down Nico. And I was prepared to do whatever I had to do. After all, I had literally killed for him, so the least he could do to repay me was to wife me.

CHAPTER 23

Nico

I had been secretly paying drug money to one of the local mega-church preachers turned politician. I was paying fifteen thousand dollars in cash every month just so I could be included as a silent investor in a group of well-known business people who were pooling their resources together in order to develop the first casino in Queens County. The State of New York was accepting bids from different developers for the right to develop and operate the casino. Seeing that my political preacher connect was the right-hand man of New York's black governor, it was all but guaranteed that our group was a lock to get the contract.

When we were finally awarded the contract, I'd have to shell out two million in order to get a two percent ownership share in the casino. It was an investment risk that I definitely felt was worth taking, simply because the potential rewards were huge.

The only thing I hated about being involved with the deal was the fact that I had to hobnob with all kinds of politicians at various fundraisers and different events taking place throughout the city. But I did what I had to do to get where I was trying to go.

I no longer had the worry of finding a new drug connect, since it looked like Bebo's plan for us to eat with the other crews was working out. We now did have the best product on the street, so from that standpoint, I was in a good space. I still didn't trust Bebo, but I knew I had to get back to making the moves I needed to make for me to permanently leave the streets alone. And the way I saw it, this casino move was the move that was going to legitimize me and get me to exactly where I wanted to be.

"What's up, baby?" I said to Jasmine, who had called me.

"Nothing. I'm chillin'. Just seeing what you up to," Jasmine stated.

I explained to her that I was going to get fitted for a new tailored suit I was planning to wear to the political fundraiser coming up in a few days.

Jasmine sounded as if she had just woken up. Her voice was groggy, and she didn't sound enthused or even the least bit impressed or intrigued by what I had just told her, in terms of me planning to attend the political event.

"So what you doing on Thursday night?" I asked.

"You tell me."

"Roll with me to this political event," I told her.

Jasmine agreed to go with me to the event, but then she asked me if I wanted to hang out with her later that night at a spot in the Bronx called Sofa Lounge. I had never been to the spot before, since I rarely hung out in the Bronx, so I figured why not. But I definitely wasn't going to go there without some of my boys.

"Yeah, we can do that," I said to Jasmine.

"OK, cool. So let's bounce around ten."

"No doubt."

"And, just for the record, you be on that bullshit," Jasmine jokingly said, her voice still sounding groggy and somewhat hoarse.

I had just finished teasing her and saying that I hoped she knew how to hold a real conversation with politicians and professional people. I laughed and told her that I would see her later.

Later on that night, I had BJ drive me to pick up Jasmine. We drove in BJ's black Escalade along with our other man LaQuan. BJ drove, LaQuan sat in the front passenger seat, and I sat in the back. When we reached Jasmine's house, I called her and told her we were outside. Catching me off guard a little bit, Jasmine asked me if I could come inside and meet her parents. I didn't really want to, but I did it anyway.

"Yo, I'll be right back," I said to the fellas as I exited the truck and made my way to Jasmine's front door.

"Hey, babe." She kissed me on my cheek before letting me in and ushering me into her kitchen.

"Mom and Dad, this is Nico. Nico, this is my mother and father."

"Nice to meet you both." I shook her mother and father's hand.

Her dad looked a lot like the father from the old Will Smith *Fresh Prince* television show, and her mother looked a lot like the dancer Debbie Allen. Only, Jasmine's mom had much lighter skin.

"Nico, my dad is Councilman White's Chief of Staff, and I was telling him that on Thursday we're going to a political fundraiser event."

"Oh, so you're into the political game?" I said. "Now I see where Jasmine gets all of her political and economic wisdom from."

Both of her parents laughed. Her father then asked me if the event I was going to was being held at the Sheraton Hotel in Manhattan.

"That's the one," I replied.

Her father then nodded his head and slowly looked me up and down.

Jasmine's mom said, "Well, we're not going to keep you two. We know you're on your way out."

"We'll have to invite you over for dinner." Her father stood back up from the kitchen table and shook my hand.

"Definitely," I replied. "I would like that. Just let me know when."

Jasmine took me by the hand and led me toward the front door.

"OK, Mom, so we're leaving now."

Her parents both told us to be safe and to have fun, and we exited the front door.

"Sorry about that. I gotta get outta that house. They stay in my business," Jasmine said to me.

"Nah, that's cool. It's good your parents are still together, and they look happy, and they seem cool. You lucky. A lot of people wish they had that. I wish I had had that."

We both got into the truck, and I introduced Jasmine to LaQuan, since she already knew BJ.

"Nice to meet you," Jasmine said to LaQuan.

LaQuan made a joke about his name, and Jasmine laughed. Then she told him not to worry, that she was good with names.

"You look good," I whispered in Jasmine's ear. "Keep that pussy wet for me."

She smiled and looked at me and nodded her head. I was definitely impressed that she was coming across very reserved and ladylike, similar to Mia's disposition, and not once did she seem like she was only twenty years old.

I whispered in Jasmine's ear, "We gotta go shop for that X6 next week."

Jasmine had been playing her position perfectly, so I wanted to at least reward her for going through with the hit on Shabazz.

"Stop playing," Jasmine said to me.

"I'm dead-ass."

Jasmine hugged me real tight and kissed me on the cheek. She couldn't stop smiling and telling me thank you.

After about twenty-five minutes of driving, we reached Sofa Lounge.

"Yo, I know this spot." BJ turned down the music. "This is the old Jimmy's Bronx Café."

I had been to Jimmy's Bronx Café back in the days, but it had been so long ago, I wasn't sure if BJ was right or not. He was probably wrong because he was the type that always emphatically knew shit but was always wrong and would never admit it. He was still my nigga for life, though.

After we parked the truck, the four of us walked toward the spot, and as we walked, I started to remember having been there back in the days.

"This is Sofa Lounge? Yo, BJ, this is where we was at that night when Stephon Marbury rolled up flossing in the drop-top Bentley and cats ran up on him at the light and made him run his shit." I laughed, remembering the incident.

"That's what I'm saying. We was at Jimmy's that night. This is the same spot. They just changed the name."

The line to get into the spot wasn't crazy, but I was never one to stand on lines. And, plus, LaQuan was a Newark, New Jersey cop, so he had his badge and always could get us in spots if there were ever any issues. I didn't like putting him in a position where his job would be in jeopardy if something ever jumped off. So I never rolled with the expectation of using the power his badge granted him, unless it was for minor shit like this.

After LaQuan flashed his badge and the bouncer let him inside, he held the rope open for us.

I handed the bouncer a hundred-dollar bill.

"Good looking out," he said.

I nodded my head to him as I cupped Jasmine by the waist, and we all walked into the spot together. The spot was cool, and was full of Spanish dudes and Spanish chicks.

A Spanish hostess asked Jasmine, "Do you want to put your coat in coat check mami?"

Jasmine took off her coat and revealed the form-fitting dress she had on. She was also rocking a hot pair of stilettos. After we had taken care of the coats and jackets, we headed to the bar and ordered drinks.

By the time we had our third round of drinks, the spot had gotten really packed. A different DJ took over, and he was much better than the first DJ, so it wasn't long before the spot was really rocking.

Jasmine grabbed me by the hand and pulled me toward the dance floor, which wasn't far from the bar at all. "You and that too-cool-to-dance shit."

"Nah, you know I just two-step," I said directly into her ear.

"You know how to fuck, so I know you can dance," she shouted into my ear over the music.

"Oh, so that's the prerequisite?"

"Something like that," she replied as I two-stepped and she danced in front of me.

ERICA HILTON

I turned my head to see if I could locate BJ and LaQuan. I wanted them to try and get a table for us in the VIP section. Before I could locate my boys, I was met by what felt like a hurricane—Hurricane Mia, to be exact.

Mia pushed me. "So you out partying with this bitch, huh?"

Mia was dressed to kill, looking like a million dollars, in a form-fitting dress and stilettos of her own. I had to quickly get things under control.

"Mia, calm the fuck down," I said.

Jasmine stepped up to Mia. "Watch who you calling a bitch!"

Mia was much taller than Jasmine, but Jasmine wasn't about to back down.

Whaaaack!

Mia smacked the shit out of Jasmine, and it looked as if Jasmine didn't expect to get hit.

"Bitch, I'll beat your mu-tha-fuck-in'-ass!" Mia said, stressing every syllable, and uncharacteristically coming across like a chick from the hood. She then began unleashing a series of right hooks that all connected with Jasmine's head. "I told you not to fuck with me!"

Jasmine screamed in anger and also to summon strength from her body. She rushed Mia and pushed her a few feet backwards, until Mia fell on the ground. Jasmine quickly took off both of her shoes and, towering over Mia, who was still on the ground trying to get up, began pummeling her with one of her stilettos.

"Get the fuck up, bitch!" Jasmine said, stomping Mia.

Then, to shoot a fair one, and feeling really amped and confident in her hand skills Jasmine relented, so Mia could get to her feet. That was a bad move on Jasmine's part. In the midst of the mayhem, Mia's home girl, Sharmel, discreetly handed Mia a knife that she had in her

Gucci bag. Sharmel then caught Jasmine off guard and grabbed hold of her. Sharmel did her best to hold on to Jasmine in the full nelson position so Mia could cut and stab her.

"Stab that bitch!" Sharmel commanded her best friend.

Jasmine wiggled and wormed and kicked desperately, trying to free herself of Sharmel's grip, as Mia approached her with the knife. Mia jigged the knife two times inside the dark club but she missed her target both times. She had to be careful because she didn't want to stab Sharmel by accident. By this time the incident had started to get the attention of everyone in the club.

I grabbed Mia's wrist and twisted as hard as I could.

"Ahhhhhh!" Mia screamed, and the knife fell to the ground.

I kicked the knife across the floor.

"Get off of me, Nico!" Mia screamed.

Whack! Whack! Whack!

I smacked Mia three times as hard as I could, and she fell down, covering up, expecting to get hit again. I yanked her up from the ground and screamed, "Quit your bullshit, Mia! And get your silly ass outta here. Now!"

"Nico don't be fucking hitting on her like that!" Sharmel said to me and she pushed me away from Mia.

"You gonna beat my ass over this trick?" Mia asked as Sharmel came to her aid.

Jasmine knew I had her back, so she began looking for her shoes. BJ came by my side, and LaQuan took Jasmine by the hand and was trying to lead her out the club just as club security was making their way over.

"Mia, shut the fuck up!" I barked. "I'm not gonna tell you again!"

Mia shook her head. Disheveled and trying to gather herself, she said some things under her breath. Then she smiled an embarrassed smile and directed her words at Jasmine.

"It's all good, sweetie, 'cause he gonna beat your ass and fuck other bitches the same way he did me. Watch!" she said, checking her nose for blood.

Jasmine hurled spit in Mia's direction as LaQuan continued to yank her out of the club.

BJ tapped me on the arm. "Let's get outta Dodge."

I had the illest screw face plastered on at the moment. There wasn't any way Mia just happened to coincidentally be at the same club as us. She must have followed me to the spot, which infuriated me. Nevertheless, I heeded BJ's words, and we bounced.

When we made it to the truck and pulled off, Jasmine kept apologizing to me.

"Baby, I'm so sorry, but I just had to defend myself," she explained.

"It's all good. You a'ight?"

Jasmine was breathing heavily and she looked disheveled and amped while telling me that she was OK.

"That's all that matters then. That bitch and Sharmel were outta line jumping you like that," I explained, trying to calm Jasmine down.

"Nico, what's good? You wanna head to the crib or to Queens or what?"

"Take me to the crib."

As we drove out of the Bronx and headed toward Long Island, I quickly had to take stock of things in my head and figure out exactly how I was going to deal with this situation. Mia may have been out of line but she had enough information about me to have my black ass sent away for double life. So, yeah, I had some thinking to do and some decisions to make.

CHAPTER 24

Jasmine

As we drove toward Nico's crib, I kept replaying the fight in my head. I was thinking about what I did good, and what I could have done better. All the while I was replaying the fight in my head, I could feel Nico's cell phone vibrating on my thigh. I had my legs stretched across him as we sat in the backseat of the truck, so I felt every vibration.

Nico didn't even look at his phone. I knew it had to be Mia. She was texting and calling him like she had lost her damn mind. That's how I knew it had to be her. No one else would call anybody like that.

After seeing Nico put the smack-down on his chick, I knew there was likely never going to come another time like the present one for me to lock him in. I had to make my move to secure my position.

When we reached Nico's sprawling mansion, BJ and LaQuan made some quick small talk, and LaQuan told me that it was nice to meet me in spite of the drama that had unfolded. I told him likewise and told them both that we had to hang out again real soon.

Even though I had been to Nico's crib before, I was still blown away by the spiral staircase, the granite floors, the stainless steel appliances, the flat-screen TV and the whole nine. He tried to get me to make myself comfortable, but I thought it would be a smarter move to leave the crib, just in case Mia showed up. Not that I was afraid of her, because I wasn't. But I wanted to get Nico alone, so that I could enact my plan and let him know about the video of Mia and Kelvin.

"Baby, I love your crib," I said to Nico. "But, listen, please don't take offense, but I really gotta get back to Queens."

"For what?" Nico asked. "Don't worry about Mia. She ain't coming in this house tonight."

I knew Nico was probably in the mood for some pussy, and I had no problem giving him any, but I had to put my priorities above his penis. I walked up to him and gave him a hug and a kiss.

"Can we just leave? I'll talk to you when we get in the car."

Nico looked at me, and then he kissed me and told me that it was no problem, that we could head back out.

He set the house alarm, and we made our way to his four-car garage, where we hopped into a grey BMW. I think it was a 750 BMW, but I wasn't sure. The automatic garage door lifted up, and we made our way out and headed to the Long Island Expressway.

"You gotta wake up in the morning or something?" Nico asked.

I was quiet as I looked at Nico. Then I reached forward and turned down the volume on the mix tape CD.

"I don't have to wake up early. I just wanted to leave because I know you live with Mia and I didn't want her coming to the crib and me having to deal with no drama," I explained, trying my hardest to come across like I was mature and taking the high road.

"Jasmine, let me tell you something. That shit that went down in the club, that wouldn't go down in my crib. I got too much nice shit up in there, for one thing, I don't play that shit anyway, and Mia knows that. She would never go there like that in my crib."

I remained quiet and just listened, waiting for the precise moment to say what I had to say.

"Something else is on your mind," Nico stated. "Speak to me."

I slowly shook my head, and my eyes began to well up. I wanted to come across as convincing as possible.

"What you saw tonight, that is so not me at all. Baby, I just wanna be with you. No drama, just me and you."

"You with me right now, right?"

"Yeah, I know, but that's not what I mean."

"So speak to me."

At that moment Nico looked down at his phone. I looked and saw Mia's name on the caller ID of his cell phone. Nico didn't answer the phone, and I could see agitation in his face.

I knew that was my moment to strike. "Call her back and tell her you wanna be with me," I said with all seriousness.

"I ain't gonna answer the phone. She'll get the message."

I shook my head and looked at Nico. "Call her and tell her the wedding is off."

"What you saying?"

I sat up and wiped the tears from my eyes. I spoke directly to Nico, so he would know I was serious.

"Don't duck Mia. Just call her back and tell her you wanna be with me and that you're calling the wedding off. I need to hear you say that."

"Jasmine, it's not that serious."

"Baby, to me it is. I'm out here fighting and shit over you, pulling triggers for you, so I need to know how you really feel."

"How I really feel? You didn't see what the fuck I just did to that bitch for you?"

We were getting close to Queens, and I wanted to hurry up and close the deal, before I showed Nico the video I had. "Baby?" I said with a whining tone.

"I'll call her right now."

"Put the phone on speaker," I replied, knowing Nico could read between the lines.

Nico reached for his phone, scrolled to the call screen, and called Mia.

"How you gonna just ignore my calls after some shit like that?"

Mia didn't even say hello when she picked up the phone. I could tell she was on the verge of crying.

Nico was quiet.

"And now you just gonna call me and be quiet on the phone. No apology or nothing, right?"

Nico still was quiet.

Mia sucked her teeth. "Baby, where are you?"

"I'm driving."

"Nico, where are you? We really need to talk."

"Mia, listen, I could tell things was going this route over the past few months—"

"'Going this route'? What are you talking about?"

"Mia, the wedding is off. I'm with Jasmine now. The shit might sound cold or hurtful or whatever, but shit been fucked up between us for a minute. You know that, and I know that."

"Nico, what are you talking about?"

Nico didn't respond, and now Mia clearly could be heard crying.

"Ain't no need for all the tears and shit. It is what it is."

"It is what it is, huh?" Mia asked through her tears.

"Yeah, no wedding, no more us, it's a wrap."

Both Mia and Nico were silent.

"Nico, let's just talk when you get home, because I'm confused and I'm missing something."

"You ain't confused, and you ain't missing shit. And I don't want you in my crib when I get there!"

Mia continued to cry. "No. I'm not going anywhere," she said.

"Mia, I'm not gonna play fuckin' games with you over this!"

"I ain't playing games either! I just want you to talk to me, Nico!"

Nico was about to say something, but then Mia cut him off.

"I know what this is," she said. "You ain't serious. You just with that chickenhead bitch right now, and she told you to call me and say this shit."

"What the fuck are you talking about?"

Mia shouted into the phone, "Nico, I know she listening. Bitch, if you listening, I ain't going anywhere, and I'll keep beating your ass until you get the point."

Nico reached over and put his hand on my thigh, for me to just chill and remain quiet. "Mia, I'm alone, so shut the fuck up 'cause you really sound stupid right now."

"Oh, now I'm stupid? You know what?" Mia sniffled. "I NEVER thought you would go out like this and do this to me, not in my wildest dreams."

Nico was quiet.

"And you going to stay on that silent bitch-ass shit, right?"

Nico kept his mouth closed as I continued to listen in. On the inside, I was beaming and doing back-flips from happiness.

"Fuck you, Nico! And you can have your young, dumb-ass ho! All that shows is how dumb your black ass is. You going to pick that bitch over me? And yet you going to call me stupid? Sweetie, let me tell you something. When you lay down with dogs, you get fleas, but when you lay down with whores, there ain't no telling what you might get. So thank you, Nico, for doing me a favor, 'cause I can tell you one thing—That bitch that's sitting right next to you now listening to this phone call, she ain't who you think she is. What's her name, Jasmine? That's what you think her name is, Nico. But ask her right now what her *other* name is. Jasmine, I know you can hear me, so why don't you tell your new man what your other name is?"

Nico gave me a confused look.

My heart started pounding. I knew she would go there when I asked Nico to call her but it was a chance I had to take. Although, I didn't want shit going here until I showed Nico what I had to show him. But I played things off and looked at Nico and shook my head and held both of my hands out to indicate I didn't have a clue what she was talking about.

"Oh, now she going to sit there all quiet and shit like a church mouse, but up in Sofa Lounge she had all the mouth in the world. Talk that Sofa Lounge shit now, Jasmine. Or should I say *Chyna*? Chyna, talk that shit now, *china doll.*"

I panicked, and I think it was evident to Nico, who silently mouthed words to me asking, what she was talking about.

Once again I shook my head and silently mouthed back to him that I didn't know.

"Quiet as a fucking church mouse! Speak up, Jasmine—I mean, Chyna—and tell Nico how you be all over Craigslist and the Internet selling your ass! Talk that shit now and tell him!"

I took my right hand and waved it from side to side in front of my neck and whispered to Nico that she was lying.

"Nico, that video-ho pussy you fuckin', it's pussy that everybody done had. So if you want to go out like that and rock with that chick, then OK cool, go ahead and do you, and I'm going to do me." Mia laughed.

"Mia, what the fuck are you talkin' 'bout?" Nico asked.

"Oh, now you want to speak? What am I talking about? I'm talking about how you need to do your homework, baby. But then again, I could be wrong. I mean, I know you been shelling out that dough to that preacher dude for that casino shit, so maybe your chips are low right now and you want some of that bargain-basement pussy. Jasmine . . . oh, I mean, Chyna, what is it that you charge again, one hundred for a half an hour and one hundred and eighty for a whole hour? Yeah, Nico, if that's what you on, then sorry. This pussy right here ain't no Wal-Mart pussy. This is high-end, exclusive, passport pussy right here, and you got to come correct, and ain't no two ways about that shit."

I sat there and shook my head. I was trying to send a signal to Nico that it was sad that Mia would lie on me like that.

Nico just looked at me, his jawbone tensing up.

"What you got to say now, Nico?" Mia asked.

"I ain't got shit to say. You sound like a bitter bitch."

Mia laughed. "And you sound like a nigga in denial. But you know what? You can lie to yourself and create your own reality, that's cool, but pictures don't lie, and the truth don't need no defense. If you want proof, I'll get you your proof!"

I couldn't take it anymore, and at that point I had to speak up. "Mia, sweetheart, this is Jasmine, and, yes, I been sittin' here the whole time listening to everything."

Mia chuckled. "So then tell him, *Chyna*, how you be selling your ass on the Internet!"

Nico was looking at me, and I could tell that he was mad as shit because I had spoken up, but I didn't care.

"No, what you need to do is tell Nico about the nigga that was banging your back out when you flew down to Miami. That's what you need to do, instead of lying on me. And if you say pictures don't lie, then videos *definitely* don't lie!"

Nico looked at me, and then he spoke right behind me. "Mia, what the fuck is she talkin' 'bout?" he yelled.

Mia paused before she spoke, and right then and there, I knew I had her.

"She ain't talking about shit. She just don't want me to show you these pictures I got of her ass, so now she making up shit. Nico, I want to show you these pictures. That's all. I want to see the look on your face when you see how much of an ass you are. Who the fuck in their right mind trades in Maybach pussy for a used, beat-up rent-a-car that everybody done literally rode in and drove into the ground?"

Nico didn't respond.

"Back on that quiet shit?" Mia asked Nico. "Fuck you! You clown!" Then she abruptly hung up the phone.

By this time we had reached Queens and were sitting in front of my crib. Things hadn't exactly played out the way I'd wanted them to with Mia mentioning pictures, so I knew I had to do some serious damage control. And the best way to do damage control was to back up what I had been saying.

"I don't know what the fuck she is talkin' about, but I ain't *never* sold my ass to *anybody*. That's just some delusional, desperate shit she is spewing right there," I said to Nico.

Nico took both of his hands and ran them down his face, sort of like he was stressed. "Look at me," he said.

I sat up and looked him right in the eyes.

"There's not an ounce of truth to what she was saying, right?"

"Baby, no! Urggghhh! My God! How could you even ask me that, Nico? You know what? Bye. I'm going in the crib to sleep. I'll call you tomorrow." I reached for the door handle to let myself out of the car, but I knew Nico wouldn't let me leave.

Nico grabbed me by the arm to prevent me from leaving the car. "Jasmine, I'm about to wife you, so I'm asking because I need to know what's good. I know how Mia thinks and how she moves. She'll pay private investigators to find out who you are and all that, and when these dudes start digging, they start finding shit. So I'm just saying, come clean with me and don't have me wifing you and I later find out some shit. Because word up, take this how you wanna take it, but I swear on everything, if you on some double-life, double-person shit, and you break my heart, I'll have your ass murdered! That's straight the fuck real talk right there."

My heart was pounding, I was repeatedly tapping my right foot, and my head felt like it was going to explode. On one hand, if I told the truth, I would spare myself any drama down the road, but if I told the truth, there wasn't a chance in hell that Nico would even call me again. If I lied, I would have a great chance at being with him because as he had just said, he was going to wife me.

The only wildcard was Mia and the information she had on me. She knew about my secret life as a prostitute, but I had no idea how the hell she knew. And if there was one thing I had learned in my short years, it was that it wasn't so much what you knew that could hurt you, it was what you didn't know that could later come and bite you in the ass.

I decided to roll the dice and hide the truth. "Baby, you can trust me. She's lying," I said to Nico, tears coming to my eyes.

"That's all I need to hear." Nico let go of my arm. "Now what the fuck is this Miami shit you was just talking about?"

I sighed and I sucked my teeth. "See, I wasn't gonna say nothing because I didn't know if it was my place to say something."

"What are talkin' 'bout?"

I could tell Nico was on edge. I pulled out my phone, went to the video, and played it. I fast-forwarded it, so I could get to the part with Mia actually fucking. Then I handed the phone to Nico.

Just sitting there watching Nico was like literally seeing somebody transform. Nico had a look on his face that scared the shit out of me. I really thought he was going to put the car in drive and go find Mia and choke the life out of her.

"Where the fuck did you get this?" Nico screamed at me.

"Kelvin sent it to me."

Nico handed me the phone and asked me how long the video was, and I told him that it was about an hour long. Then he asked me to forward it to his phone. I told him I would have to e-mail it to him, since it was a big file. Then he gave me his Blackberry e-mail address, and I sent it right to him.

"Yo, I gotta go," Nico said to me.

I leaned over and gave him a kiss on the lips.

"Nico, I did want to tell you about the video but I felt it wasn't my place . . . and I didn't want to hurt you. I know how you feel about her."

Nico nodded his head, but he didn't say anything to me.

ERICA HILTON

I exited his car and went straight to my bedroom, where I pulled out my laptop and got right on the Internet. I had one goal for that night, and it didn't matter how long it took me. I was going to make sure that anything and everything related to my prostitution activities was deleted from the Internet.

My heart pounded insanely as I covered my Internet tracks. I was thankful that I had never shown my face in any of the online ads I had posted. But my tattoos were visible in many of the online photos that I'd posted. If Mia had printouts of any of the ads that showed my tattoos, my ass would literally be toast in Nico's eyes.

The anxiety I was feeling was ridiculously overwhelming. I wanted to smoke some weed to calm me down, but I didn't have time for that as I feverishly logged on to different web sites and deleted anything and everything related to Chyna.

After I deleted everything, I had calmed down a little. I sat and thought that, no matter what Mia produced, I was going to continue to lie my ass off and never admit to shit. If Nico were to question me about any pictures with tattoos, I would say that it was just a coincidence, that it wasn't me in those pictures.

Was I totally confident? No, I was not. But I was determined. I was determined to bag Nico and take him away from Mia. I was on the verge of achieving my goal, with just one small hurdle left. I knew guys never played that "sharing-the-pussy-that-they-are-wifing" bullshit.

Women could overlook and forgive a lot of shit, but with men, once they know you fucked someone else while you were with them, it usually was a wrap. I was just hoping that it was indeed officially a wrap for Mia.

CHAPTER 25

Mia

My heart was in my stomach when I hung up the phone with Nico. Right away I called Sharmel.

"You OK?" Sharmel asked me as soon she picked up the phone.

"No I'm literally dying right now. Oh my God!" I was uncontrollably trembling with fear.

"Mia, what happened?"

"Tell me the truth and be totally honest with me. Did you tell Ricky *anything*, about what happened down in Miami with me?"

"Hell, no! Are you crazy? I would never tell him no shit like that. He would be looking at me sideways if I did," Sharmel replied.

I knew that she wasn't lying. "Nico knows about Kelvin," I said, desperate.

"Nooooo! How?"

"I have no idea, but that fucking bitch Jasmine was telling him that she got me on tape with a nigga in Miami banging my back out."

"She's fuckin' lying, Mia."

"So then how would she even remotely know to say something like that?"

"Kelvin's from New York, and it could be a coincidence that she recently spoke to him. Don't stress out."

"Sharmel, she was down there in Miami! Fuck! I knew I saw that bitch down there." I started crying.

"Mia, she wasn't down there. Calm down. That's just your mind playing tricks on you. All you need to do is tell Nico that you met Kelvin and he was an owner of the club and he got us in the club and bought us drinks, and that's it. Nico knows you, so he ain't gonna believe you would step out on him like that."

"OK, I guess you're right. I just wish I had listened to you and not fucked that dude. What the hell was I thinking?"

"Mia, that's in the past. You're human, and you were really going through it. Things happen. Don't beat yourself up."

I sighed into the phone and thanked Sharmel for listening to me. I asked her to keep her phone on, just in case I had to urgently call her back.

After I hung up the phone, I went to my computer and printed out what I had saved of Jasmine's ads.

I tried to calm down. I still wanted to make sure that I was coming across confident, so I sent Nico a text and asked him, was he coming home to the apartment so I could show him what I had to show him.

Nico didn't respond, and I looked at that as somewhat positive because, had he really had wind of me fucking Kelvin, there was no way he would have remained silent on that.

About a half an hour later Nico came home. He slammed the door so hard, I thought he broke the locks.

I grabbed the printouts I had of Jasmine and ran to the living room to meet Nico and show him my evidence. "Here's your—" I said and tried to hand him what I had.

Whack!

Nico hauled back and slapped the shit out of me to the point where I literally saw stars, and I fell backwards until my back hit the living room wall and blood trickled out of my mouth. Then he charged me and grabbed me by my throat and started choking me with one hand. He was applying so much pressure, I just knew he was going to crush every bone in my neck.

"You went down to Miami to fuck some nigga!" he screamed at me. He was so angry, he couldn't get his words out quick enough and was spitting on me while he yelled.

I was still seeing stars from his initial powerful slap and felt like I was about to pass out, but I kicked and scratched and swung and did everything I could to free myself from Nico's ninja-like chokehold grip.

"Who the fuck was that nigga?" Nico demanded to know.

I tried to shake my head no, but as angry as Nico was, he had to have known what went down. He flung me halfway across the living room floor.

I was in such pain. I reached for my throat, gasping and coughing, desperately trying to get some air into my lungs.

Nico ran up to me and started kicking and stomping me, and all I could do was scream, since there was no way I was going to physically force him to stop beating me.

Just then the building's concierge came running into the apartment to see what was going on. He let himself in with the master key.

Nico looked up and saw our concierge, Harry, towering over him. "Everything is a'ight!" Nico yelled to him.

"Help me," I said. I was certain that Nico was about to kill me.

Harry pushed him away from me, telling Nico to calm down and to just try to relax, and that nothing was worth getting locked up over.

Nico's chest was visibly rising and falling. Then he spat in my face, and it landed straight in my eye.

"Nico, come outside with me for a moment," Harry said to Nico, trying to get him to leave the apartment. "The neighbors will call the police if this continues. I told them I could handle it. My job is on the line if you don't stop this insanity."

Harry was a reasonable man. He'd worked as a concierge for nearly twenty years and sent his only son to an Ivy League school on tips alone. He knew how to turn a blind eye for the rich. And although he knew he should have called the cops on Nico for hitting his woman, the tip for *not* calling the cops is what his bottom line was.

"So you're siding with that whore?" I wiped Nico's spit from my face. "You won't even look at what I printed out, because you're in denial!" I said, grimacing in pain.

"Give me one minute. Just step outside for one minute," Nico said to Harry. "You got my word, I ain't gonna touch her again."

Harry seemed torn but he gave in to Nico's request and stepped out of the apartment, he left the front door open.

Nico retrieved his cell phone from the living room floor. It must have fallen to the ground when he was kicking me. After scrolling through the phone, he pressed a button and showed the phone to me. Instantly I recognized myself in the hotel room getting fucked by Kelvin.

"You see this shit?" Nico asked me.

"Nico, give me the phone!" I tried to grab it out of his hands, but he pushed me off and held me at bay while I tried to take it from him.

As we tussled, I could no longer see the images of Kelvin fucking me, but I could hear everything I had said totally out of character for me, and my words made me cringe from embarrassment.

"Fuck me harder, you black muthafucka! . . . Pull my hair and fuck me deeper! . . . You like this wet pussy? . . . Smack my ass!"

"Now you gonna tell me that ain't you?" Nico asked me.

"Nico! Baby, you don't understand!" I said, tears streaming down my eyes.

"What is there to fuckin' understand? Tell me right now why I shouldn't murder you behind this stunt?" Nico hollered at me.

I went up to Nico and tried to hug him, but he shoved me across the room, sending me crashing into a picture that was hanging on the wall. The picture fell to the floor and the glass frame shattered.

Harry came back in the apartment to see what was up.

Nico told him, "Yo, she's leaving! Get her the fuck up outta here right now! Otherwise, I'm getting locked up for murder tonight."

"Nico, I'm not leaving until you talk to me," I said through tears and immense anger.

"Take her ass out right now."

Harry gently grabbed me by the arm.

"Get off me!" I shouted and flung my arm free. "Nico, everything we had, you just tossing it aside over this?"

"You should've asked yourself that question before you flew to Miami to fuck that nigga!"

"God please help me!" I screamed. "This is sooooo frustrating, because that's not what happened!"

"So while I was calling you and texting you, you was fuckin' that nigga, and that's why you was ignoring me, right? Get the fuck outta my crib! And, like I said, consider yourself lucky you still fuckin' breathing!"

Harry came up to me and tugged me, forcing me to go with him as I wailed and cried.

"This is not happening! That bitch caused me to lose my man! I don't believe this shit!" I said out loud.

Nico shouted, "No, you caused this, Mia! Nobody forced you to open up your legs!"

"OK, I'm coming with you," I said to Harry. "You don't have to pull on me."

Harry took me to the elevator and explained to me that he was just doing his job. "Is there someplace you could stay the night?"

I closed my eyes and bowed my head. I just paused for a few seconds because I felt like I was going to explode.

"I've seen these domestic violence situations before, and trust me, things escalate. So it's better to leave the house now. In a day or two, no matter what it is, it can be talked out. But if you don't walk away now, then emotions get more involved and common sense goes out the window, and the next thing you know, things happen that somebody ultimately regrets. You understand?"

I nodded my head. Then I asked Harry if he could go inside the apartment and get my bag with my car keys.

After he got the car keys for me, I got inside my truck and started the ignition. I sat for about five minutes with the engine idling. Then, right before I pulled off, I sent Sharmel a text: *Nico showed me a video of Kelvin and I fucking. It's over for me.*

CHAPTER 26

♥

Jasmine

I t had only been six weeks since Nico dumped Mia and put her ass out. And within those six weeks, he had moved me in to live with him in the lap of luxury in his sprawling Long Island estate. Even though I had moved in with Nico, I was still in school for nursing. I had a longer commute to Brooklyn every day from Long Island, but it was OK because I got to commute in style in the brand-new all-white X6 that he'd bought for me.

Although I was enjoying the luxuries that came with being wifey, I was wondering just what had I walked myself into by wanting to be Nico's main girl.

Within the three weeks I had been living with him, two different chicks came by the house looking for him while he wasn't home. Both of the chicks had the same story and wanted the same thing. They both claimed that they used to mess with Nico and that he had gotten them pregnant, and they wanted to know what he was going to do about supporting his child.

None of the chicks was ghetto or stank in terms of how they spoke to me, so it made me think that there was a lot of truth to their stories. And because they weren't stank with me, I wasn't stank with them. But at the same time I was smart enough to know not to trust no chicks. I didn't tell Nico that they came by. Let him find out on his own and clean up his own mess.

See, not too long ago I was the woman on the outside looking in, trying to get on the inside with Nico, and now that I had that position, there was no way I was going to give any woman even an inch with my man. Because, after all, it was only an inch I needed to bounce Mia out of the picture.

Truth be told though, the women who came by the house were not really my main concern. I was more worried about the cops and the federal agents who came knocking at our front door on several different occasions. But I really got alarmed the last time the feds came by looking to talk to me specifically.

I was just heading out the door and ready to go to school when two homicide detectives met me at the garage door.

"Excuse me, Jasmine," one of the detectives said to me. "Do you mind if we talk with you for a moment?"

They had flashed their badges, so I knew they were legit. What had me nervous was, they knew me by my first name.

"Well, actually, I'm in a hurry, kind of late for school, so I don't really have too much time. But I can give you a few minutes." I didn't want to totally brush them off and make myself look worried about something.

One of the officers took out a pen and a small pad. "OK, we appreciate it. So, Jasmine, do you know why we're here?" he asked me.

I was no dummy, and Nico had coached me well on how to talk to the feds and to the police. An innocent person is always direct and never vague, while a guilty person is always vague and rarely direct.

So that was why I wanted to be as direct and clear with my answers as possible.

"You're trying to find out information on my ex-boyfriend Shabazz," I said.

The agent nodded his head as he looked at me, and then he said, "We've interviewed a lot of people about Shabazz's death and the drugs found inside his vehicle at the time of his death, and the pieces are falling together quickly. If you had anything to do with his murder, you should come clean and make it easier on yourself."

"I don't know anything about how he died, or who was involved, or why there were drugs in his truck."

"Did you know any of the people Shabazz associated with on a regular basis?"

"You mean, his friends?"

"Yes, his friends or associates."

"Well, yeah, of course."

"Was Nico friends with Shabazz?"

"Yes," I said, and then my heart started to beat.

"And what is your relation to Nico?"

"Just friends." I wanted to bounce, but I didn't want them to think that they'd pushed the right buttons.

"Was Shabazz OK with you and Nico being friends?"

"Of course. I was cool with everybody Shabazz was cool with and vice versa."

The agent scribbled down everything I was saying, and then he asked me, "Who do you think would've wanted to kill him?"

"That's something I think about a lot. I don't know. Shabazz was a street person, so I just said to myself that it's unfortunate, but that's just how it is. It's sad."

I knew I had given the detectives more than enough of my time, so I told them that I didn't mean to be rude, but that I had to bounce because I had a quiz I couldn't miss.

The detective handed me his card and thanked me for my time.

"If you hear anything about Shabazz's death or the drugs that were in his truck, give me a call," the detective said, "regardless of what it is or how insignificant it might seem."

"OK, I'll do that," I said and I walked off.

"You're a nursing student, right?" the detective asked.

"Yeah," I replied and continued on into my car.

As I started up the car and pulled out of the garage, the detective stopped me. I rolled down the window to see what else he wanted.

"Do yourself a favor. You're a beautiful girl. Focus on your education and start your nursing career. Leave this world alone. Trust me on that," the detective said. He was an older black guy, about my father's age, and the way he came across just reminded me so much of what my father would tell me.

I just looked at the agent and didn't say anything, and I drove off to school. I wasn't going to say anything to Nico about the detectives questioning me because I didn't want him to think I wasn't built for his world.

Later that night I said something because I was worried. Nico assured me that I had nothing to worry about because the agents had nothing to work with.

"Remember, babe, when they got you, they come to lock you up. When they don't have nothing, they come by just fishing for information, and then they bounce. They were just shaking the tree to see what falls out of the tree. You're good. We're good." Nico kissed me on the forehead.

Nico went out of town the next day. He told me that when he got back, he would take me out to a Manhattan restaurant and start spending more time with me.

It was all good because I had midterms to study for, so it gave me the undistracted time I needed to get ready for my exams.

I should have known that the peace and quiet I was enjoying wouldn't last for long. As soon as Nico got back in town, I started to get text messages from Mia. But I knew that the best thing I could do to infuriate her was to simply ignore her, and that was exactly what I did.

Then early in the morning on the day that me and Nico were planning to go to dinner, I got another text from her:

You went from mistress to wifey, but you're going to soon know that I AM wifey!

Oh, this bitch is so annoying! I said to myself after reading her text. *Let it go, bitch, and move on! Dayum!*

I wanted to text her back, but I continued to ignore her.

Later that day, at around eight o'clock in the evening, me and Nico found ourselves inside Mr. Chow's in Manhattan. Right after we were seated the waiter took our order. Out the corner of my eye I spotted two men in suits walking up to our table. I don't know why, but my heart started pounding.

I was asked, "Are you Jasmine Sinclair?"

I was speechless.

"Yeah, her name is Jasmine. Can we help you?" Nico stood up. "We tryin' to enjoy a night out."

The two men flashed their badges. One spoke, "NYPD homicide unit. We're placing Ms. Sinclair under arrest for the murder of Samuel "Shabazz" Barton."

"What?" I asked in disbelief.

"Turn around and place your hands behind your back."

"Nico, help me, please . . . "

Nico looked helpless.

"Baby, I'll be on the phone with my lawyer in five minutes. Don't worry about nothing, and don't say nothing to these niggas until the lawyer gets there."

The detectives placed handcuffs on me and prepared to cart me outside as everybody inside the restaurant looked on.

"Oh my God!" I screamed in anguish. I couldn't believe this was happening. "Why are you doing this to me?"

"It's our job," one detective replied, sarcastically. "We lock up murderers."

"I didn't kill anybody!" I pleaded.

"Jasmine be quiet!" Nico warned. "Don't say anything else until your lawyer gets there."

Tears were on the verge of streaming down my face, but I wanted to be as strong as I could in front of Nico. I didn't want him to see me crying and think that I would fold under questioning. As the detectives led me out of the restaurant the only thing I could think of was Mia's last text message to me. I did go from mistress to wifey.

But at what cost?

Keep reading for an excerpt of

WIFEY:
I AM WIFEY

PROLOGUE

Jasmine

I was hauled off to Midtown South's police precinct and all the way there my heart palpitated from fear. *What have I gotten myself into?* I wasn't brought up this way. Not to be charged with murder at twenty years old. As we passed by yellow cabs, bright city lights, and numerous pedestrians, I realized I wasn't going down without a fight. No one saw me do shit, and I wasn't going to admit shit. I'm going to sit with a poker face, and if that didn't work, I'd resort to tears.

The marked police car pulled around to a side entrance and I was led out the cramped back seat by the taller detective. No one said a word to me as I stoically held my head up high. The police precinct was a stark contrast from the eerie silence I'd just experienced. The noise and chaos jolted my senses, and instantly I became jittery. I began to fidget, turning my wrists uncomfortably in the handcuffs until they became irritated.

"Could someone loosen these cuffs?"

Instead of accommodating my request, I was shoved, slightly, from behind. My pressure instantly rose, but I didn't dare lash out.

I was on their territory and realized, quickly, that I was way out of my league.

Eventually I was escorted to a back room that looked cold and sterile. It had the quintessential desk and two chairs that you see on every cop television show. As the two detectives began to have small talk amongst themselves, I was handcuffed to a chair and then left alone.

At first, I was relieved that they didn't come back into the room to question me. I figured that Nico had hired me an attorney and the detectives were given strict orders to back off. But as the minutes turned into an hour, which turned into hours, I got restless.

"Hello?" I called. I waited a few seconds and elevated my voice. "Hel-lo!"

Where was everyone? Why had no one come back into the room to check on me? I continued to call out, angrily, until I got tired. Eventually, I put my head on the desk and fell into an uncomfortable sleep.

Hours had passed when I was awoken by a female officer who took me to the ladies' room and offered me something to eat or drink.

"When am I being processed?" I asked. I just wanted to see a judge who would hopefully set a bail and I could go home to my warm bed. "I've been here for almost ten hours. And where's my attorney?"

She shrugged. "I don't know anything about your case. Are you sure you don't want anything from the vending machine? Soda? Chips? Nothing?"

Who could eat when you're about to be charged with murder?

"Nah, I'm good. Thanks anyway."

A couple hours after sunrise the door burst open and two middle-aged white gentlemen in jeans and button-up shirts came walking in. They both had intense eyes and a confidence that intimidated me.

"Jasmine?"

"Yes?" I replied, meekly. The fourteen-hour stint had broken any bravado I thought I possessed.

"We're transporting you to another location." He then bent down and unclasped my handcuff. "Turn around and place your hands behind your back."

"What? What's going on? Why am I being moved?"

No matter how many questions I asked, none were answered. As I was led through the precinct, it seemed that we had the attention of everyone. I couldn't understand why all eyes were on me, unless it was purely my imagination. And where was Nico and my attorney?

This time we drove to lower Manhattan and went through an underground parking garage near Reade Street. I was led to an underground elevator where the man had to use a key card for entry. We rode up 27 floors and once again I was placed into a room. I had no idea where I was, but it seemed like I was in an office building as opposed to a police precinct. After around ten minutes, the door reopened with one additional person, a black female. Everyone took nearby seats and a tape recorder was turned on.

"Jasmine, I'll cut straight to the chase. My name is federal agent Dowd and these are my colleagues, Agent Battle and Agent Kelsey. We've taken over your case from the state police in the hopes that you'll be smart and help yourself."

The moment he said he was a federal agent I began to drift in and out of lucidness. *Why are the feds interested in me?*

Agent Dowd continued, "You will be indicted for the murder of Samuel 'Shabazz' Barton, and we will most certainly tie you into a conspiracy to distribute narcotics which will upgrade you to a RICO charge. Those charges alone carry a minimum life sentence. And if you know the federal government's track record for successfully prosecuting cases, which is 98 percent—you'll help yourself. So, think about your odds of beating the case before you tell us your answer."

"But I didn't—"

The black woman, agent Battle interjected.

"Jasmine, we're only going to make this offer once. And we don't tolerate lies. We know you killed Shabazz in the iHop parking lot and we also know your boyfriend, Nico got you to do it. We're not going to explain what evidence we have, but just note that we rarely take over state cases unless we are one hundred percent certain we can win. You're a young, beautiful girl. Think about spending the rest of your life behind bars."

I was afraid to open up my mouth to protest my innocence. "You guys just pluck me out of the precinct violating my civil rights? No attorney, no phone call, nothing? My parents don't even know where I'm at! That's kidnapping! While I'm doing time y'all need to be in a cell right next to mine. How is this even legal?"

Ignoring my slight outburst, agent Dowd continued. "We've had surveillance on the Ghetto Mafia crew for over five years. They're going down with or without you."

Finally agent Kelsey spoke, and I didn't like what he had to say. "We need you to help put Nico behind bars. And I know what you're thinking. You're thinking about how much you love him. But better yet, you're thinking about how much he loves you. You're remembering all the expensive gifts he gave you—the BMW, watches and furs. Guess what? All that's being confiscated. But what you should think about is that you've only been in here less than twenty-four hours, and your Nico has already hooked back up with his ex-girlfriend, Mia."

Agent Kelsey pulled out a few glossy photographs of Nico meeting up with Mia. One photograph showed both cars parked side by side. In the next, she'd hopped into his truck. The next, they were walking into our residence together.

"This doesn't mean shit," I replied, defiantly.

"Of course it does. It means that you *can* easily and *will* easily be replaced. You're already a memory. It's every man for themselves. You don't honestly think that he'll do this bid with you? Come on visits for the next seventy years of your life? Send you birthday and Christmas cards? Do you really think that?" He paused, and then continued. "Save yourself. No one will know that you're working with us. On that I give you my word. No one will know. And once this is over and done with, you can find yourself another Nico to buy you the finer things in life."

I exhaled. I knew one thing and that was I ain't no snitch. But it wouldn't hurt asking a few questions.

"What would I have to do . . ."

SHEISTY CHICKS
BY KIM K.
DECEMBER 11, 2011

**BAD APPLE
BY NISA SANTIAGO
NOW AVAILABLE**

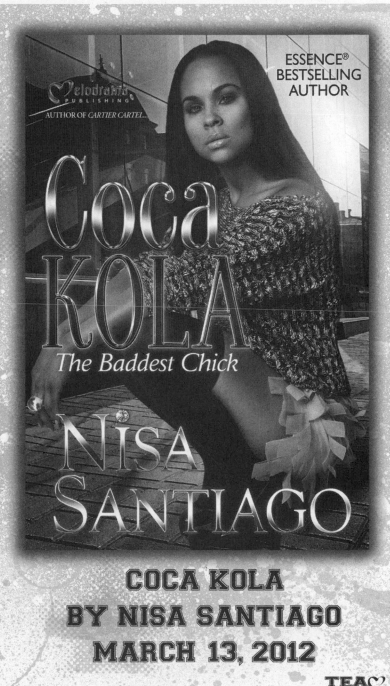

COCA KOLA
BY NISA SANTIAGO
MARCH 13, 2012

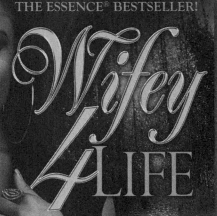

THE ESSENCE® BESTSELLER!

Wifey 4 LIFE

"Kiki captures the
heat of the streets."
—Wahida Clark,
New York Times Bestseller

Kiki Swinson

WIFEY 4 LIFE
MASS MARKET EDITION
BY KIKI SWINSON
FEBRUARY 14, 2012

TEA♡
MELODRAMA

Melodrama Publishing Order Form
WWW.MELODRAMAPUBLISHING.COM

Title	ISBN	Qty	Price	Total
10 CRACK COMMANDMENTS by ERICA HILTON	978-1-934157-21-3		$15.00	$
BAD APPLE by NISA SANTIAGO	978-1-934157-45-9		$14.99	$
CARTIER CARTEL by NISA SANTIAGO	978-1-934157-18-3		$15.00	$
CARTIER CARTEL MM by NISA SANTIAGO	978-1-934157-34-3		$ 6.99	$
COCA KOLA by NISA SANTIAGO	978-1-934157-48-0		$14.99	$
DEAL WITH DEATH by ENDY	978-1-934157-12-1		$15.00	$
DIRTY MONEY HONEY by ERICA HILTON, NISA SANTIGO, KIM K	978-1-934157-44-2		$14.99	$
DIRTY LITTLE ANGEL by ERICA HILTON	978-1-934157-19-0		$15.00	$
DRAMA WITH A CAPITAL D by DENISE COLEMAN	978-1-934157-32-9		$14.99	$
EVA II: FIRST LADY OF SIN MM by STORM	978-1-934157-35-0		$ 6.99	$
I'M STILL WIFEY (PART 2) by KIKI SWINSON	978-0-9717021-5-8		$15.00	$
IN MY HOOD by ENDY	978-0-9717021-9-6		$15.00	$
IN MY HOOD MM by ENDY	978-1-93415757-2		$ 6.99	$
IN MY HOOD 3 by ENDY	978-193415762-6		$14.99	$
JEALOUSY: THE COMPLETE SAGA by LINDA BRICK-HOUSE	978-1-934157-13-8		$15.00	$
JEALOUSY by LINDA BRICKHOUSE	978-1-934157-07-7		$15.00	$
LIFE AFTER WIFEY (PART 3) by KIKI SWINSON	978-1-934157-04-6		$15.00	$
LIFE, LOVE & LONELINESS by CRYSTAL LACEY WINSLOW	978-0-9717021-0-3		$15.00	$
LIFE, LOVE & LONELINESS MM by CRYSTAL LACEY WINSLOW	978-1-934157-41-1		$ 6.99	$
MENACE by MARK ANTHONY, AL SAADIQ BANKS, J.M. BENJAMIN, ERICK S. GRAY, & CRYSTAL LACEY WINSLOW	978-1-934157-16-9		$15.00	$
MYRA by AMALEKA MCCALL	978-1-934157-20-6		$15.00	$
RETURN OF THE CARTIER CARTEL by NISA SANTIAGO	978-1-934157-30-5		$14.99	$
SHEISTY CHICKS by KIM K.	978-1-934157-47-3		$14.99	$
SHOT GLASS DIVA by JACKI SIMMONS	978-1-934157-14-5		$15.00	$
A STICKY SITUATION by KIKI SWINSON	978-1-934157-09-1		$15.00	$
STILL WIFEY MATERIAL (PART 4) by KIKI SWINSON	978-1-934157-10-7		$15.00	$
STRIPPED MM by JACKI SIMMONS	978-1-934157-40-4		$ 6.99	$
TALE OF A TRAIN WRECK LIFESTYLE by CRYSTAL LACEY WINSLOW	978-1-934157-15-2		$15.00	$

MELODRAMA PUBLISHING ORDER FORM
(CONTINUED)

THE CRISS CROSS MM by CRYSTAL LACEY WINSLOW	978-1-934157-42-8		$ 6.99	$
THE DIAMOND SYNDICATE by ERICA HILTON	978-193415760-2		$14.99	$
WIFEY (PART 1) by KIKI SWINSON	978-0-9717021-3-4		$15.00	$
WIFEY 4 LIFE (PART 5) by KIKI SWINSON	978-1-93415761-9		$14.99	$
WIFEY 4 LIFE (PART 5) MM by KIKI SWINSON	978-1-934157-43-5		$6.99	$
WIFEY: FROM MISTRESS TO WIFEY by ERICA HILTON	978-1-934157-46-6		$14.99	$
YOU SHOWED ME by NAHISHA MCCOY	978-1-934157-33-6		$14.99	$

Instructions:

*NY residents please add $1.79 Tax per book.

**Shipping costs: $3.00 first book, any additional books please add $1.00 per book.

Incarcerated readers receive a 25% discount. Please pay $11.25 per book and apply the same shipping terms as stated above.

Mail to:

MELODRAMA PUBLISHING

P.O. BOX 522

BELLPORT, NY 11713

Please provide your shipping address and phone number:

Name:_____

Address: _____

Apt. No: _____ Inmate No: _____

City: _____ State: _____ Zip: _____

Phone: (   ) _____-_____

Allow 2 - 4 weeks for delivery

Bulk orders call 347-246-6879 FOR DISCOUNTS